Pianotown

for Heather

Pianotown

Russell Helms

first edition

ISBN: 978-1-943661-32-9

sij books

booksbysij@gmail.com

Please inquire for rights and reproduction.

Cover image: Adobe Stock images

Against all odds, a few of these stories have previously appeared: Meat Drying in the Sun (*Litro,* as Hairspray); Killing Seahorses (*Unbound Walls*); Theme Park (*GFT Press*); What God Looks Like (*Le Scat Noir*); You Must Be Born Again (*Trench Foot Gazette*).

Contents

Lick the Knife

Rhea gazed at the ice through the kitchen window. A wolf paced in the frozen yard eager to eat her. The gas oven yawned a tunnel of heat that spread across the room. She fumbled in the silver drawer for a knife and cut her thumb. She kicked a box of oatmeal cookies in the floor and said, "Dammit to hell."

The next day she went outside and moved the cement birdbath, first the fluted bowl and then the matching stand. Bits of seed, berries, and stringy brown algae sloshed beneath the skim of ice onto her rubber boots. She stepped on a can of hairspray hidden in a tangle of garden hose. Beneath "Do not spray into eyes" she read this: "In order to thwart the wolf you must think like an Esquimaux." She puffed her menthol cigarette and threw it into the snow.

While making tomato soup from a can, she began to think like an Esquimaux. She gathered the steel needles in her house and put them in a safe place. She took a length of pig's intestine, stripped out the gelat-

inous lining, and filled it with egg yolks,
which she then buried in the yard. She
called all of her friends and forbade them to
utter her name, for it was very unlucky in
the far north for one's name to be spoken
aloud.

That night the wolf visited again and
came to the back door, pressing its fangs
against the glass. Rhea stood still, becoming
one with the furniture until the wolf, puz-
zled, ran away into the cold night to rum-
mage for pizza crusts and slops of canned
tangerines.

Rhea spread pelts of polar bear on the
hardwood floor and lit a blubber lamp. The
lamp crisped and cracked sending forth a
deep pale of yellow into her living room. She
envisioned heaving ice, igloos, puffins, auks,
and the dark liver of a freshly killed seal.
She slept well.

The next day, Rhea removed her gloves
and hammered a strong wooden stake into
the hard ground where the birdbath had
been. From her sealskin boot, she pulled a
double-edged knife, razor sharp, and bound
it to the stake using caribou sinew. She spit
onto the wrapping, freezing the cord and
securing the blade.

She skipped lunch and upon a bearskin
pallet gave birth to a son. She held it by the

ankles, carried it outside, and watched its breath catch in the biting air. There was no more soup and being the dead of winter and being alone and thinking like an Esquimaux she hung the child from its neck and ate it raw, saving the belly fat to grease her boots.

That night the wolf returned and finding a shank of meat posted upon a stake of wood began to lick the frozen blood. The wolf licked and licked, feeling warmth gather upon its tongue as the taste of meat caused its stomach to roar with hunger. With each lick, the knife sliced deeper into the wolf's tongue, the flow of its own blood becoming ever greater. The wolf grew dizzy and snapped at the air. Rhea watched it stagger into the night, pleased that she would see the wolf never again.

Meat Drying in the Sun

Pianotown smelled like hairspray. The court house was yellow and wrapped in vinyl siding. Summers in Pianotown started cool in the morning but climbed to heat stroke by noon. As always, Scarlet Hodges dragged her crooked body round and round the plastic baby pool.

Two weeks into the long days of summer, Scarlet dreamed of her brother. She dreamed that Pal jumped too high on the trampoline beneath the powerline and in a clonic spasm popped and crackled for a period of sixteen hours. The trampoline jutted just over the edge of the pool, her only shade.

The very next day, Pal jumped too high on the trampoline, spied the drooping cable, and grabbed it because he could. He smelled hairspray. A hum of current cinched his hands around the line and rippled his jaws. He saw the distant yellow court house as a filmstrip caught in a fan.

Scarlet frowned. Brown cars with vanity plates passed on the way to the yellow court house. A blind man tapped the sidewalk

with a raspy cornstalk. Scarlet slapped the
water, slapped the water. He paused and told
her not to be wasting water, that it was summer. He lingered. He'd heard Scarlet was
pretty.

As the days passed, the water in the pool
darkened to pale yellow and irritated Scarlet's legs. The burns on her shoulders and
face festered. She lay still in the tiny quar-
ter-moon of shade beneath the lip of the
trampoline. Pal hung limp, black, and dry on
the powerline.

The blind man scratchity scratched up
the sidewalk with his cornstalk. He smelled
ammonia, hairspray, and meat drying in
the sun. He listened for the sounds of a
ten-year-old boy named Pal jumping on a
squeaky trampoline. "Hi there little crooked
girl," said the blind man. "Are you eating
some meat dried in the sun?" He kicked a
can of hairspray. He listened. He moved his
stalk toward the ammonia smell.

Scarlet pushed against the pool and
slunk. The yellow water ate into her shoulders. She trembled, ecstatic and terrified.

That evening at seven, Scarlet's mother
limped home from the hairspray factory and
found the blind man drowned in the pool.
She rearranged the hairspray cans in the

yard. Scarlet wouldn't let go of the blind man's cornstalk so she let her keep it.

Tommy Thornbottom read on the side of a hairspray can that a blind man went to heaven. He waited for the brown cars to pass and walked across the narrow street that led to the yellow court house. He picked up a hairspray can and read about Pal drying in the wind above the trampoline.

"What's your name?" said Tommy.

Scarlet lay on her back in the baby pool. The dark water tickled the bottom of her knees. She held tight to her cornstalk.

Tommy picked up a hairspray can and read that her name was Scarlet Hodges, that she was the crooked girl who spent summers in a baby pool. "I've read about you," he said. "Can I jump on the trampoline?"

Scarlet struggled to sit up. The night before, she'd dreamed that Tommy Thornbottom would take her cornstalk. She reached over the side of the pool, grabbed a can of hairspray, and held it out to Tommy.

Tommy read, "By all means, Tommy Thornbottom, be my guest and jump on the trampoline. You want to take my cornstalk, but why not jump on the trampoline first?" He thanked Scarlet, jumping higher and higher. He saw the sagging powerline and some meat drying in the sun.

That night around seven, Scarlet's mother limped home with a bag of hairspray and a bag of old bread she'd found at the duck pond. She hand-fed Scarlet a few crusts and placed cans here and there in the yard. She smelled fresh meat dried by the sun. A fire truck raced by on its way to a grease fire and she waved.

This Town is Cancer

Near the yellow county court house sat the brown city jail. Near the brown city jail lived Lisa Dreamdaré.

"Hello, father? Are you still in jail?" Lisa looked out the window at a fringe of razor wire. She could almost reach out and touch it.

"Yes, dear, that's why I'm calling. I've decided that I love you more than sliced bread and would like to memorialize you on my skin." He perused graffiti in the phone booth. *Pianotown sucks. Smell my finger. This town is cancer. Work from home.*

Lisa pinched a tuft of cat hair to the backdoor and set it free. It was difficult to speak with her broken jaw. "Do you mean you would like a tattoo of my face, perhaps on your chest?"

"Yes, exactly, or perhaps a tattoo illuminating your laborious handwriting would be better." He bent down to examine a can of hairspray. The label read, "Your daughter is a fool and deserves to die."

"Oh father, I'll do it if you promise to

love me again. Will you, father?" Lisa's hip brushed the kitchen table and the whole thing collapsed. A cup of warm water doused the yellow kitchen carpet.

"What I need you to do, honeycakes, is this. Write your name on a piece of paper and put it in the mailbox. I'll have my good friend Sharla bring it to me here at the jail. Of course, that means you'll have to come out of the house." He crossed his fingers. A small dirty dog urinated on the phone booth.

Lisa looked for some paper. "Are they treating you well, father? Did you enjoy the cookies I sent over. They were oatmeal. I remembered to leave out the nuts."

"Listen, what would be really neat, would be for you to write your name, in cursive of course, on the back of a blank check. That way you'd be sure and write neatly and compactly. I think that's a great idea."

"You know my writing hand is broken, father. May I print with my left?"

In the booth outside the hairspray factory, the phone dangled by its cord.

Gut Racing

James (Dr. Hartman) gathered his keys and wallet for a trip to the Variety Store, needing things such as sturdy fishing line, a lead weight shaped like a lozenge, and two sturdy eyehooks. The man duct-taped to the kitchen table in his living room didn't weigh so much, and that was good. James (Dr. Hartman) needed some soft cheese as well, perhaps baby Swiss.

"I'll be back," said James (Dr. Hartman).

The man on the table nodded. His mother had never given him a whole stick of gum, just half a stick, and now this.

James (Dr. Hartman) pulled the door closed and wrapped a bit of wire around a nail to keep it shut. He noted the smell of meat drying in the sun and said "Hello" to the little crippled girl in the baby pool. He picked up a can of hairspray and read about the hitchhiker named Eddie Cavanaugh who was duct-taped to his table. The man would soon die a slow horrible death, first swallowing (words jumbled) attached to a lead weight until it passed through his gut.

Down the crooked sidewalk James (Dr. Hartman) went. He smelled cookies. Brown cars puttered by. He glimpsed the yellow court house. He saw a wad of keys and hesitated. One of the keys looked familiar. He remembered the man taped to the table and moved on.

The man taped to the table raised his head and gazed down a row of shirt buttons to his splotched brass belt buckle. Everything seemed to be in order. He smelled hairspray.

"You're kidding me," said James (Dr. Hartman) to Gleason.

"You'll need piano wire, not fishing line," said Gleason. He owned the Variety Store. He handed James (Dr. Hartman) a can of hairspray.

James (Dr. Hartman) read aloud, "Fishing line is not sufficient to saw through a carcass, even from the inside out. What someone needs to do is buy thin piano wire instead."

"Have a good one," said Gleason. He handed the bag of piano wire, a lead weight shaped like a lozenge, and two sturdy eyehooks to James (Dr. Hartman). "Don't forget the soft cheese." He winked.

~

There was a Catholic Church in Pianotown, but no one attended. The other church, the Unitarian, wasn't really a church. It was a fellowship.

Boistrous Rainey—everyone loved her name—led the fellowship each week in song and introduced the week's speaker. It was kind of like taking classes at a New Age junior college, but without the diploma or student loans. Boistrous was a retired faculty member from the nearby private college, Tock University, where she had taught marketing for some twenty-five years. She knew her Four Ps—product, price, place, and promotion—and consulted part-time at the hairspray factory just a few blocks away.

Boistrous led the assembly in a simple song about the basic things in life and then told an anecdote about flipping her brother's four-wheeler when she was young and killing her cousin. She ate carrot sticks while she talked. It was that death that had caused Boistrous to leave the Catholic Church and begin her search for why bad things happen to good people. Surely, God wasn't so cruel. She acknowledged the presence of the priest, Father McGlawn.

The speaker that Sunday was a Feldenkrais Method practitioner (Dr. Hartman) who was also a Baptist Buddhist. Boistrous looked out to the audience, the shimmery gray hair, the worn corduroy jackets, plain dresses with turtle brooches, and clean sneakers.

"Welcome," said Boistrous. She was a large woman with broad shoulders and a long nose. She wore a violet skirt with a loose white men's shirt and sandals. "We've all seen today's speaker, Dr. James Hartman, riding around town on his single-speed bicycle. And some of us know what good wine he makes. Yum. Let's welcome him."

There was a light scattering of applause.

"Thank you, Boistrous," said James (Dr. Hartman). He smelled lemons and perhaps pipe tobacco. "Today, I'd like to talk about my experiments on a hitchhiker I picked up over a month ago. As we speak, he's duct-taped to my dining-room table and..."

The door to the "sanctuary" opened and an elderly couple entered, both wearing sweaters from the 1970s.

"...a thin piece of piano wire, over thirty feet in length is making it's way through his intestines." James (Dr. Hartman) noticed a couple of hands raised and paused to take questions.

"How did you get him to swallow the piano wire?" said a man with cancer.

"Good question," said James (Dr. Hartman). "Basically, I attached a small lead weight to the end of the piano wire and wrapped it inside a piece of soft cheese to make it easier to swallow."

"I see," said the man with cancer.

"Another question?" said James (Dr. Hartman).

"On average, how far does the piano wire advance each day?" The woman asking was in her thirties. She made jewelry from fossilized animal poo.

"After the lead weight passed into the small intestine, I'd estimate that the piano wire has been advancing at a rate of six inches per day. The small and large intestines are roughly twenty-seven feet long."

"Can you do the math for us?" asked a teenager dressed like a wizard from Harry Potter.

"Well, I'm no mathematician…Perhaps we should defer to Dr. Pinky in the back." James (Dr. Hartman) chuckled.

Dr. Pinky gripped the folding chair in front of him and stood. "Well there are twelve inches to the foot, that would make 324 inches, divided by 6 that would be 54 days for the wire to emerge from the hitchhiker's rectum. I hope I'm using the proper language."

"That sounds about right," said James (Dr. Hartman). "Another thirty days or so and I'll see the lead weight, shaped like a lozenge, emerging from, as Dr Pinky stated, the 'hitchhiker's rectum.'"

"That's curious and fascinating," said Boistrous.

James (Dr. Hartman) nodded. He took a paper towel from his pocket and blew his nose. "And now let's talk about the Feldenkrais Method of somatic education."

"That's what I'm here for," said the priest. He rubbed his hands together as if presented with a sumptuous meal.

~

As predicted at the Unitarian "Church" by Dr. Pinky, the lead weight attached to the piano wire emerged from the hitchhiker's anus on the fifty-fourth day. The hitchhiker sold insurance, never bothered a soul, and had a wife and two grown children. His Dodge Dart had broken down and James, (Dr. Hartman), had given him a lift from the interstate.

James (Dr. Hartman) waited a few more days until there was as much wire coming from the hitchhiker's mouth as from "down there." And then the experiment began. To get started, he let the famished hitchhiker sip a can of strawberry Ensure laced with crushed Dilaudid.

The two eyehooks were already in place in the basement, one on either side of the cement-block room, placed about six inches from the floor. The floor was tile and had been waxed to a blistering shine by James (Dr. Hartman). He didn't want friction to impede his studies. He struggled with the hitchhiker, dragging him by the arms to a red polyurethane mechanic's creeper. He lay the hitchhiker on his back and began to duct-tape him firmly to the wheeled cart. *Skriiik* tear! He had to hurry before he woke up.

The hitchhiker awoke and his free arm swung like a baseball bat, catching James (Dr. Hartman) on the chin. He fell backward. The hitchhiker screamed, but his taped mouth was filled with pillow foam.

James (Dr. Hartman) grabbed a tire iron and cracked the hitchhiker's skull. A dark blue bruise rose across the man's cheek and right orbit. Bright blood stained his teeth and trickled from his mouth. The hitchhiker's name was Eddie. Eddie Cavanaugh. His parents had been missionaries in El Salvador. He was naked, except for the duct tape. The otherwise empty room smelled like coconut shells, a combination of concrete and floor wax.

James (Dr. Hartman) dusted himself off, just like in a movie. To each end of the piano wire, he affixed a wire leader of four feet, three inches. He attached each wire leader to an eyehook and removed the slack. Now would be a good time to put a feeding tube down Eddie's throat, so he did that. He would vary the feedings to see if the hitchhiker's speed across the floor varied. If the hitchhiker vomited, would reverse intestinal motility make him move backward? Who knew?

~

quick recap: Dr. James Hartman, a Feldenkrais Method practitioner has abducted hitchhiker Eddie Cavanaugh and duct-taped him to a mechanic's creeper in his basement. James (Dr. Hartman) has fed a thin piano wire through Eddie's digestive tract. The wire extends from Eddie's mouth as well as from his anus. Each end of the wire is attached to an eyehook on either side of the room. There is no slack in the line. The muscular contractions of Eddie's intestines pull him slowly along the wire across the room, about six inches per day. James (Dr. Hartman) pushes Ensure and water through a feeding tube in Eddie's nose. The room now smells like diarrhea, even with the diapers, which James (Dr. Hartman) must change two or three times a day.

~

James (Dr. Hartman), thin and with a limp, descended the narrow wooden stairs into the concrete-block basement. He eyeballed the day's progress, a good inch since he last checked. The hitchhiker, Eddie, who is thinking of the stray dogs at his trailer that need to be fed, as well as his wife and children, watched James (Dr. Hartman) with crazed eyes. His back ached and he felt the skin wearing away from his buttocks and neck. The feeding tube has caused weeping sores in his nose. He can't scratch, can't move, and the fluorescent light blinds him. He's been cold for the past week and shivers.

"What you need is a friend," said James (Dr. Hartman). I may invite some people over from the Unitarian 'Church' to sit and talk with you if that's okay."

Eddie tried to nod his head Yes and made his eyes say, "Great idea!"

Meanwhile, James (Dr. Hartman) got lucky and picked up another hitchhiker, a robust woman named Pearl. She had been waiting at a bus stop and just hopped in like a puppy when James (Dr. Hartman) drove up, like it was the natural thing to do. Pearl was headed to the strip mall on the other side of the highway but didn't mind a "little detour" as James (Dr. Hartman) put it.

Once inside James's (Dr. Hartman's) 1930s' California Bungalow, he let Pearl interact with his pet iguana, Hermosa. He then clubbed her on the back of the head with an aluminum baseball bat and hefted her heavy frame *thud, thump, thud* down the basement stairs. He would duct-tape her to the floor near the far wall and let her watch Eddie as he progressed inch by inch via intestinal motility across the floor. The plan was to pass a piano wire though Pearl as well and let the two race.

"Eddie, this is Pearl," said James (Dr. Hartman). "Pearl, Eddie."

The piano wire attached to the lead weight took only fifty-one days to pass through Pearl's gastrointestinal tract. Either her intestines were shorter than Eddie's or her intestines were more powerful. She seemed to be having trouble breathing, her lungs sounding a bit wet, so James (Dr. Hartman) propped her up with a foam wedge before he duct-taped her to the mechanic's creeper. Duct tape was not cheap, and the foam wedge cost $42.99. Not to mention the adult diapers.

The doorbell rang and James (Dr. Hartman) answered. He ushered in the Flybetters, an elderly couple from the Unitarian "Church." He prepared mint tea and led the Flybetters into the basement. Mr. Flybetter was a tall, gangly fellow with a swish of white hair. His wife was somewhat shriveled but still had a pretty smile. The Flybetters surveyed the plain room. They both wore combinations of orange and brown. There was only one chair, a red diner chair.

"This is Eddie." James (Dr. Hartman) pointed to Eddie, who had a red 3 painted on his chest over the duct tape. "And, I'd like to introduce Pearl." Pearl's number was 28. Her large breasts were taped to her sides. Both Eddie and Pearl mumbled through the tape across their mouths and made desperate pleas with their eyes.

Mr. Flybetter let his wife take the chair. He poked at the ceiling, a drop ceiling with acoustic panels. He then asked a series of questions about how James (Dr. Hartman) fed his "racers." Did he bathe them? Just their private areas was the response. Mrs. Flybetter wanted to know what air freshener scent he was using in the basement. Lilac was the reply.

"More tea?" said James (Dr. Hartman).
He placed the hot kettle on Eddie's stomach.

"No, thank you," said Mr. Flybetter.
"Pretty interesting set-up you've got here."

"Well the races can't begin until more
wire emerges from between Pearl's buttocks.
I plan to invite a few people over, perhaps in
a week."

"I see," said Mrs. Flybetter, disappoint-
ment rimming her voice. "Well, old man,
let's be going." She clutched her black purse
to her chest, ready to drive to the grocery
store and buy some moist cat food.

~

Father McGlawn, somewhat skeptical of the
whole affair, followed Boistrous into James's
(Dr. Hartman's) house. He liked the little
fireplace to the left with the built-in book-
shelves. Cracks ran through the old plaster
walls.

"Welcome," said James (Dr. Hartman).
"Today is the day of judgment." He had
read that earlier on a can of hairspray, while
fetching a newspaper from the corner store.

Boistrous smiled. A platter of carrot
sticks and raw almonds sat on the dining
room table. "Well, I'm excited to be a part
of this. I'm sorry more couldn't make it.

There's the double whammy of an antique car show *and* an improv poetry festival."

"Competition," said James (Dr. Hartman), "is what greases this country's wheels."

Father McGlawn ate an almond and secreted a few into the folds of his maroon robe. Why was there always a crowd at the Unitarian "Church?" It didn't make sense but neither did he consider himself an old dog. Perhaps he could learn some new tricks, and this gut racing sounded cruel but interesting.

James (Dr. Hartman) retrieved a bottle of homemade wine from the cabinet in the butler's pantry. The bottle was cloudy glass and made the wine seem like pig's blood. After pouring three Dixie cups of wine, they made their way to the basement.

The scene was set. On one mechanic's creeper in the middle of the room lay Pearl. Her eyes looked like blown lightbulbs. She seemed to be in a coma. Two feet away was Eddie. He still had some life in him. He tried to sit up, scream, shake his head, kick his feet. Duct tape is strong, though.

"My goodness," said Boistrous. "This is one waxed floor." She surveyed the pair of hitchhikers with piano wire emerging from their mouths on one end and from between their legs on the other.

Father McGlawn was silent.

"Well, let's get going," said James (Dr. Hartman). He sipped his wine. "Any friendly wagers? Of course, I'm biased, so you may want some insider information."

"Pearl is fatter than Eddie," said Boistrous. "Does that mean her intestines are perhaps longer or fatter even?"

"Hmm," said James (Dr. Hartman). He pondered the logic of Boistrous's question. "Just because clouds are white doesn't mean they're made of milk."

Father McGlawn drained his wine and placed the cup on a metal TV tray.

James (Dr. Hartman) took a roll of silk tape and placed a strip in front of each mechanic's creeper just in front of the wheels. This was the starting line. Whoever traveled the farthest in the next hour would be judged "the winner."

"To make things more interesting, I'm going to push a can of expired strawberry Ensure along with a bottle of magnesium citrate down each feeding tube," said James (Dr. Hartman). He put on a pair of latex gloves and prepared his egg timer. He asked Boistrous to push the liquids down Pearl's tube while he took care of Eddie. Twist went the egg timer, *tick, tick,* and the race was on.

During the intervening hour, the three discussed why it was so hard to keep children attending the Unitarian "Church."

"Well, everyone is so old to begin with," said Boistrous. At forty-eight she was a youngster in the "Church."

"Do you think the pagans scare the children?" said James (Dr. Hartman). "They wear those wild outfits, sometimes without underwear."

Father McGlawn agreed. He thought the pagans were freakish. They all lived together in a commune, but they were friendly, especially the young lady with pointy ears like an elf.

Before you could say "skin the cat," the egg timer rang its awful ring. The race was over. Both racers, their diapers full of liquid stool, looked exhausted. Pearl was definitely unconscious but her bowels were in full gear. Eddie's eyes darted back and forth. He hoped he was the winner.

James (Dr. Hartman) tore another strip of tape, *skrik,* and laid it down in front of the wheels of one creeper and then the other. It was close. He took a yardstick from the local lumberyard and measured the distance between the pieces of Eddie's tape. "Looks like an inch on the dot," he said.

Boistrous and Father McGlawn watched together.

"Okay, here it is for all the marbles," said James (Dr. Hartman). On his knees and with a wrinkled nose he measured Pearl's motile progress. "One inch and five-eighths. Winner!"

A look of horror crossed Eddie's swollen face. *What next!*

~

To celebrate Pearl's victory, an announcement was made at the Unitarian "Church." There would be a potluck ceremony to be followed by the unveiling of Pearl's "prize."

Dr. Pinky brought potato salad with a precise ratio of mayonnaise to mustard. Father McGlawn brought a box of communion wafers. He sprinkled them with cinnamon-sugar to make a kind of God cookie. Boistrous could not attend, having to visit the chiropractor for her knees, but two pagans were able to make it, the one who dressed like Harry Potter and the short one with elf ears.

After nibbling "cookies" and drinking several bottles of wine, James (Dr. Hartman) led the group into the basement. He had affixed red balloons to the ceiling with pushpins. The basement reeked of lilac, feces, and urine. Since the race two days before, James (Dr. Hartman) had more less neglected the two hitchhikers duct-taped to mechanic's creepers. The fluorescent lights blinded Eddie. Pearl was no longer alive and beginning to bloat, but she was still the winner.

Father McGlawn noted the presence of two engine lifts, one at either end of the room.

Harry Potter took the single chair, bringing a great look of consternation from Dr. Pinky. The elf woman sat in his lap.

"So, how does this work?" said Dr. Pinky.

"Well, its pretty simple," said James (Dr. Hartman). "First, we cut the duct tape like this. Next, I attach this end of the wire emerging from Pearl's rectum to this engine lift, just so." He walked to the other side of the room, hooking up the wire to the second engine lift. "And like this just so. And now we lift."

Father McGlawn swallowed hard. The elf woman was bending over and her nipples were showing.

"Can I get a little help?" said James (Dr. Hartman).

"Sure," said the elf woman. Her father worked on cars, and she was handy with an engine lift. She pumped the handle up and down, taking out the slack, and James (Dr. Hartman) did the same.

"Well, here's to the winner," said James (Dr. Hartman), and Pearl's body began to lift from the floor, the wire sawing through her carcass from the inside out.

Killing Seahorses

Wednesday

Claude thought it was neat to have a head on the back of his head but not an entire human being.

"The Leffler twins…" said his brother Lawrence. Lawrence knotted his face and screwed his eyes sideways into the closet.

"Yes, I know," said Claude. "Debbie, the one with floppy legs, has become parasitic. They've strapped her to a wheeled device that Karen pushes like an IV pole."

Lawrence, the strongest, leaned forward. Claude arched backward and his foot lifted from the carpet. "Let's not wear the black t-shirt," said Lawrence.

Claude grimaced. "But the black lights look good on black. It makes us look nebulous, like we're suspended in a cloud of squid ink."

"What are you reading at the open-mic tonight?" said Lawrence. He tilted his head forward again. The strain of skull-bone felt good.

"Hey," said Claude. "Cut it out." He was

going to read a compilation of feedback comments from beheading videos on You-Tube, a kind of list poem.

"Are you taking the Valium today?" said Lawrence. Otherwise they had awful spasms in their backs and necks.

"Maybe you should start taking your own Valium," said Claude.

They crab-walked to the bathroom.

"So, what are you reading tonight?" said Claude.

Lawrence was going to read a compilation of feedback comments from Leffler twin videos on YouTube, a kind of list poem. Usually he and Claude alternated lines, improvised and all that jazz. The small but intimate crowd that gathered once a month at the Pianotown fire station open-mic loved it.

"I hope the Leffler twins are there," said Lawrence.

"I hope al Qaida is there," said Claude.

They had a good laugh and brushed their crooked teeth.

Thursday

A metallic car pulled into the Dearborn's driveway. Special Prosecutor Sparks, gloved in red, touched the car's nose to the Dearborn's garage. A man named H preceded her to the door and unbuttoned his dark blue jacket exposing a nine-millimeter Springfield XDm, a striker-fired pistol, double-action only, which was such a smooth shot that even an expert such as H might be tempted to note in an email to a friend who worked at Stouffer's managing their refrigeration technology that the gun should be reclassified as single-action.

Canon A.E. Baker Dearborn Jr. opened the door. His daughter Claire Elise Bradley paused at a piano recently tuned by a blind man who smelled of parakeets. Canon's wife Rebecca St. John Alba wiped her hands on a dishtowel patterned with three-leafed clovers.

H, followed by Special Prosecutor Sparks, pushed past Canon into the tan living room.

"What's this?" said Canon A.E. Baker Dearborn Jr.

"Probably just another one of your porno schemes, *Carlotti de Franco!*" H pounded his good fist into his other fist. "There are two PCs in this house, now where are they?"

"Do as he says," said Special Prosecutor Sparks.

"What's this?" said Rebecca St. John Alba.

"A dishtowel bearing a trefoil pattern, common in Anglo Saxon religious architecture," said Claire Elise Bradley. "I gave it to you for Mother's Day."

H barged into the back rooms.

Special Prosecutor Sparks produced an album with pictures from her summers at Bald Rock Church Camp in Chula Vista, Alabama, and gathered everyone around to kill time.

After forty-seven minutes, H reappeared. He looked pale. He'd never before seen such an extensive archive of beheading videos. He hitched his thumb at Special Prosecutor Sparks. "Let's go," he said. "We've made a terrible mistake."

Thursday Afternoon
Near the tiny island of Sindup, in the San Blas Archipelago, located off the Caribbean coast of Panama, Kuna Indian "dive guide" Moco shook the wallet out of the gringo Phil's dive bag and counted out nearly two grand in US dollars. He dumped a bucket of fresh alligator chunks over the side, hand-hauled the cement-block anchor up through aftershave blue-green water, and fired up the jerry-rigged engine. Sand sharks with their awful underbite smiles swarmed. Forty feet below the 25-foot Bertram hardtop, which had washed up after Hurricane Mitch, Mary and her parents gazed at seahorses and fan coral.

Friday

The usual crowd of experimental teenagers and retired faculty from the community college milled and slid around. The firemen were out tackling a juicy blaze-up at a chain motel, probably a grease fire someone said. A scratchy record from France played.

"I can't see," said Debbie.

Her sister Karen, known as K, shifted the pole thing that cradled her parasitic twin in a canvas sling. "Let's keep it real, okay?"

"Twenty-four seven," said Debbie.

"Sshh. Lawrence is up," said K.

"Who's the guy with the chainsaw," said Debbie. A thrill ran from an imaginary line connecting her throat (A) to her pubis (B).

"Shush."

Lawrence tugged at the turquoise collar of a thin sweater made for two heads. He rolled his neck and made Claude tilt. He took the microphone. "I'm Lawrence. The other voice you will hear tonight is that of my brother Claude, a man often known as Dangereux on YouTube."

Some kids said, "Cool." An elderly gentleman whispered, "What're ewe tubes?" On a hunch, Special Prosecutor Sparks sat in the back row. She knew the man with the chainsaw. Lawrence strained his eyes at the list poem. Claude cleared his throat.

Debbie scratched the back of her neck. Canon A.E. Baker Dearborn Jr. yanked the cord on his chainsaw, a Dolmar 7900, "the best in the business" according to the blind piano tuner. "Cool," said one of the teenagers. He wore a t-shirt with a pop-art frozen biscuit on it.

"What's this?" said Lawrence. He recognized the man with the chainsaw as Carlotti de Franco. He tried to run but there was a man attached to the back of his head.

Special Prosecutor Sparks saw that her job was done and left.

An Hour Earlier
At the orphanage north of town, an aquarium bubbled. Mary reached into the warm salty water. The seahorses' eyes grew wide. Their pipette mouths made tiny O's. Mary placed each one on a clean white washcloth. She said, "Your name is mommy and your name is daddy," and then watched them die.

Soiled Puzzle Book

Mr. Peanie reached over the head of his bed and scratched his nail against the hardening varnish. The walls were made of cardboard, sturdy cardboard that required regular shellacking to keep them from buckling, especially after a rain.

"Nurse! Nurse! I got to hock!" Mr. Peanie fumbled through his wispy clogged sheets searching for the call button. The button was white, a white box with a plastic bar that lit up yellow when pushed. It was connected to the wall by a long white cord. Yanking on the cord had caused a rip in the wall. He smelled varnish and moldy cardboard.

He couldn't find the button and just went ahead and hocked in the bed. It oozed between his legs and soiled his red paper-thin scrotum. He was reading a book upside down, a puzzle book, a word search book, and he dropped it in the mess. He adjusted his metal-framed glasses and smeared hock on the lens.

With the pressure diminished in his rec-

tum, he searched his body for a new stim-
ulus and discovered he was hungry. Had he
had breakfast? Was it day or night? It was
awful quiet so it must be night. He looked
over at his roommate, a skeleton with a
busted hip and oxygen. The skeleton mumbled into a green mask, fogging the plastic.
Where the hell was the missus, Mama Peanie?

He reached out his soiled fists and made
to clasp the face of his Mama Peanie. He
said her name several times in a raspy voice
like lemon juice was draining down the
back of his throat. Somehow the part in his
dull silver hair stayed put. He always kept a
comb in his shirt pocket, kept his hair neat
for the customers. He used to sell cars. He
would carry a small New Testament, white
with gilded edges and a pretty little red silk
bookmark, and act surprised when he caught
the eye of a customer. Why certainly! They
could interrupt his daily walk with God.
Why just look at this '63 Rambler. Ain't she
the peaches! And he would carefully mark
his place in the little Bible and lick his lips.

Someone was roughing him up. "Hey,
hey, hey now!" he said to the large figure in
white. Looked like a mattress stuffed with
cotton and two tiny arms flailing at him.

"Mr. Peanie, you done shited [with a

long i] yourself, again. Lord have mercy on us folks taking care of the likes of you." Nurse's aide Debbie Dee dropped the soiled puzzle book into the trash, which was full of half-empty Ensure cans and a pair of old turquoise houseshoes. She threw back the sheet and found a can of hairspray. In bold, small-capped letters she read this: "Unless you get your GED *and* learn how to work the microwave, your little mitts will remain soiled with the excrement of others." Debbie Dee sprayed long and hard from the can, a scent like blue alcohol.

"I got to hock," said Mr. Peanie. He cocked his head down trying to look through the smear on his glasses.

"You done hocked and you know it," said Debbie Dee. "Own up to it. You ought to be ashamed. Poor old Mr. Banana over there, or whatever his name is, putting up with you. And me too!"

Mr. Peanie's face softened. "Mama Peanie?"

"If your wife was here she would spank you for hocking in the bed, don't you think?" She rolled him on his side without putting a pillow between his bony knees, not wanting to soil the pillow. She hitched her knit pants, felt for the safety pin in the waist, and looked around for a box of gloves.

Aquarium Gravel

Doreen rakes the Kitty Kling between the couch and the TV. The dust chokes her. She lives in a fifteen-hundred square-foot litterbox and is the loneliest thing ever in Pianotown.

She climbs a stepladder to the lip of the box and exits down a set of wooden stairs built by her father so many years ago. She waves at the man named Harold across the street. He leaves a garbage can at the end of the driveway and pretends he doesn't see her.

A squirrel runs, stops, and skitters across a drooping powerline. The cat crouches. Its tail sweeps the street and two lawns. It strikes. A utility pole splinters and Doreen hurries inside the litterbox, intent on washing clothes and adjusting picture frames.

The dark gray cat with a fuzzy face tiptoes into the litterbox. Doreen presses herself to the plastic wall. The cat steps on the couch and pushes it into the chalky clay pellets. The cat turns round and round. Its tail knocks Doreen this way and that. A photo of her father falls. He smiles from an earthmover mining cat litter in Kern County, California.

At the grocery store, Food Kingdom, Doreen buys coffee and Kitty Kling. A handsome man with a mustache decorates the coffee can. A photo of her father on a bulldozer decorates the cat-litter bag. Doreen says hello to the cashier who yammers to the clerk at the next register about the price of Basmati rice in Nepal. The amount on the receipt is wrong. Doreen's been charged for two cans of coffee instead of one. But there it is, on the can, an address that she's never noticed before. El Salvador she says aloud. I don't think they grow rice in El Salvador says a cashier. How would you know says the other cashier. Do you read encyclopedias? And that puts an end to the rice conversation.

At home, in the dim shaft of light coming through the cat hole, Doreen writes a short letter to the address and signs her name. She lays the coffee can on the pillow beside her and turns off the flashlight. She wants to read but she's too excited. She remembers the day her mother was overcharged for cat litter and wrote a letter. She dreams of living inside a fifteen-hundred square foot

coffee can, of her exclusive night of love
with a mustachioed man, and of their child
who will one day be charged twice for what?
aquarium gravel?

Sprinkle Cheese

The voices told Cherie to shoot herself in the stomach. But she had to do it at the corner store called Kitty Katz where they sold sprinkle cheese and candy cigarettes. She found her father's pistol in her mother's jewelry box, which resembled a miniature rolltop desk. The pistol was black and had crosshatched grips. The engagement was off. She was eight months pregnant. Her grandmother had just died, and the goldfish had fungus.

"Jiminy crickets!"

"Shoot yourself, Cherie. In the belly!"

"Jiminy crickets!" She licked her cold sore. She was fat. Her ankles were swollen. She had a hole in her heart. The engagement was off.

There had always been the personality disorder, "on the spectrum," and so on, but she had never heard voices until now. Her fiancée had confessed that he was gay, that he had herpes, and that he wished her well otherwise.

"Jiminy crickets!"

"Do it do it do it do it…"

She walked as if caught between opposing fields of magnetism, weirdly bending. She stopped and examined a trash can on top of which sat a can of hairspray. Just above 12 fl. oz. she read, "Your name is Cherie. You deserve better."

"Poke the barrel in your gut, right in the bellybutton. Pull the trigger," said the voices. Weird radio noises, warm sun on her forearms. "Do-it. Do-it. Do-it." Her father had violated her human rights when she was seven. He worked at a fried chicken place across town, near the firehouse. He had white patches on his elbows that bled.

Kitty Katz was packed with shoppers! It was near the main road through town. They sold gas and coffee and small round mirrors. Cherie tugged down her cable-knit sweater to hide the gun in the waistband of her animal-print stretch pants. The voices moved her up and down the aisles until she was even with an end display of sprinkle cheese. A man was examining flavored waters nearby. Two children with their fists gripping bags of meat snacks edged around her.

"She's fat," said one.

"She's hallucinating," said the other.

The unborn child was the devil's. Her fiancée had broken off the engagement because of *it,* and he didn't love her anyway. She'd helped him realize he was gay. He was handsome.

Acoustic ceiling. Dolphin chatter. Gray cement floor. "Doit doit doit doit." Headache powders. Wrenches in a dryer. She stuttered. She had a birthmark on her face shaped like a cloud. The baby was possessed. The engagement was off. She had herpes. "Doitdoitdoitdoit!"

Craving clarity, she pulled the foil lid from a can of sprinkle cheese, poured some in her hand, and licked and licked.
    "Jiminy crickets!"

The Wild Horses of Kansas

from the *Pianotown Register*:
According to Celia Dupree, her ten-year-old daughter Libby led a quiet life, covered in a thick layer of fur from birth. Libby liked to read, *The Hobbit* and *Watership Down* being her favorite books.

During the night of September 21, Ms. Dupree said that she was sleeping with her husband when she awoke to strange sounds in the hall. It was Libby crawling and choking, her hairy face a shade of vegetable blue.

"Her lips were purple," said Ms. Dupree. "I screamed and my husband flew out of bed. He seemed to know exactly what was going on and ran to the garage for the needlenose pliers."

Ms. Dupree cradled her only child, "the life going from her eyes as I held her."

By the time Mr. Dupree returned, Celia had gone limp and stopped breathing. He opened her mouth and with a flashlight could see the obstruction in her throat. He inserted the pliers, pinched the tip of the hairball and pulled.

"It just wouldn't come out," said Mr.
Dupree with tears in his eyes. Celia then
began seizing, biting his hand, and breaking
a tooth on the pliers.

"I just slowly died right there with her,"
said Ms. Dupree. "There was nothing I could
do."

Weeping, Mr. Dupree stated that he had
possibly taken the wrong approach. "Now
that I think about it, I should have gotten a
wooden spoon and pushed the hairball back
into her stomach. I feel like I killed her."

County Coroner Hank Lidbetter has
ruled out foul play and considers the death
an accident.

In lieu of flowers, the Duprees ask that
donations be sent in Libby's name to help
save the wild horses of Kansas.

Storm Brew

Labrynthia Sitzbath struggled to find the floor and hold on. The roof severed, hovered, and dissolved into dust. The world roared. The wind pulled little Charlie from her arms. A piece of steel fencing drove into her kidney just above a birthmark the color of brown mustard.

~

Tony's oily perm jiggled up and down. The mulched cross-country track crunched beneath his feet. Within two minutes he passed a scrawny man with a thin beard going the opposite direction around the one-mile course. Tony said, "Howdy!" and manufactured an encouraging smile. A slight twist of wind lingered in their passing and slithered up an imaginary tent pole that held the ivory sky in place.

Doug flinched at the other jogger's Howdy! He noted where they had passed and calculated the location of their next encounter. He picked up his pace and sucked his teeth. The counseling sessions were not going well.

The wide path wound to and fro. A large pond fringed with willows, cattails, and junk trees lay at the path's far end. Rolling pasture flowed into the distance. The community college's new criminal justice building lingered along the upper reaches of the track. Near the pond, blackbirds with neon red splashes on their wings gripped branches. Robins strained to hear the language of worms. The sun lazed above gathering toothsome clouds.

Tony puffed up a short incline. He wondered if he'd locked the minivan. The clutch was slipping and it took forever getting up to 55. Probably a fifteen-hundred-dollar fix. He glanced to find the other runner, who had looked sad and frail.

Doug's wife enjoyed counseling. He'd hoped it would be enough to let her talk. But then he'd started blabbing his pie hole and couldn't shut up. It always went back to high school. His hamstring tightened as usual. His knee grabbed.

On their second meeting, Tony noticed the other guy jogging funny, like he was dragging a leg. Tony said Hey and forced an exercise grin. He noticed where they passed one another and wondered if maybe this lame older guy was on a faster pace. He stepped it up a notch and drifted back to the night at the Red Wagon. He always had the same thing, a pitcher of Bud Light. He liked to watch the college girls with his buddy Steve. Tony blamed everything on the vodka and Red Bull. A puff of air compressed between the runners, spun, and twirled skyward. A breeze raked the pond.

The cat had dragged a bleeding baby rabbit into the garage, the bunny weakly screeching for its mother. Doug looked at the ground and watched his bad leg swing forward. He imagined the other guy was too overweight to be running so hard. He let the downhill accelerate him, throwing his leg out as far as it would go.

Tony leveled onto the long straightaway that followed a barbed-wire fence. He always, always, left the Red Wagon by nine, home in time to see the kids to bed. It'd been a Friday, the end of the semester. This one chick in a silver mini-skirt had been pole dancing with a microphone stand. He'd bought her a shot of vodka and a Red Bull. She'd said he should have one as well.

The sky looked a little cloudy. A gust of wind fluttered Tony's tank top. The other jogger limped into view. Tony huffed out a half grimace and wiped his eyes.

A low bank of clouds began to layer into

a convex felt eraser. As they passed again, a
quickening draft swirled the dust.

Doug had never dated in high school,
just four years of blueballing, falling in love
with every girl he saw, afraid to masturbate even when his parents were out of the
house. First it had been jolly Santa Claus
watching him every minute of the day and
then sweet Jesus with his bloody hands.
Doug kept his pace.

To the sounds of Ernest Tubbs, this chick
in the silver miniskirt's breast had flopped
out during one of her maneuvers. Masking
tape covered her nipple, like she knew it was
going to happen. She stuffed it back in, and
that's when Tony asked her where she lived.

The first counseling session had been
totally fine. Doug's wife went through her
personal history with Dr. Sitzbath, detailed
some rough spots in her life, brought up
the fact that she had quit drinking recently.
Afterward, she and Doug had enjoyed Indian
food. But then halfway through the second
session, it'd been Doug's turn. A drop of
rain hit him in the eye.

A grumble of thunder pummeled the air
blowing at odds with itself. Tony pushed
harder. He felt the other guy coming
around the bend. Sweat burned his eyes. He
strained.

They nearly touched shoulders as they passed. Tony's chest hurt. Doug's leg felt tighter than usual. A congealed grayscale sky began to rotate around the invisible tent pole and torqued toward the middle creating a churning purple eye.

~

The guy Tony with the greasy perm left before Labrynthia woke with a blistering headache. She peeled off his pillowcase. The tape residue on her nipple clung to little Charlie's lips as he fed. Charlie looked just like her dad *Dr. Sitzbath,* and it was way too embarrassing. She wondered if a tornado could really suck a baby from its mother's arms and belched.

The Art of Conversation

With an interstate running through it, there was more than the occasional traveler who stopped in for a brew at the Red Wagon, Pianotown's watering hole. Most were drawn by the billboard, "World's Largest Cat! Twenty feet Tall!"

As is the wont of weary travelers, the conversation often turned to 1) death, 2) politics, and 3) the world's largest cat. Larry Sizemore was such a traveler, passing through on his way to Plattsville, New York, to the funeral of a beloved friend from high school, a woman called Dainty. They had dated in eleventh grade.

"She was a fine woman," said Larry to the bartender Luis Grenadine Folk Jr., who insisted on using his full name.

"Did she have gonorrhea in her cunt hole?" said Luis Grenadine Folk Jr. "You ever smell gonorrhea in a cunt hole?"

"Hmm," said Larry, lost for words. He wore a form-fitting dress shirt, loose at the collar, with a pair of knit slacks.

"Smells like fucking roadkill in the hot

sun," said Luis Grenadine Folk Jr. He leaned against the liquor case and smelled his fingers. He wore black jeans and a "See Giant Cat" t-shirt.

Larry sipped his beer, an ultra-IPA called Bitter Enemies. "How about the elections? Is there anyone worth voting for? I really would like to have the chance to just vote No. It's so discouraging."

"What I'll do is fucking get a flame thrower and whoever gets elected, I don't care who the motherfucker is, I'll incinerate them along with their whole fucking family, kids, dogs, and all. Pour acid on their corpses when I'm done." Luis Grenadine Folk Jr. tapped his fingers on the copper-plated bar. "How's that IPA?"

"Definitely hoppy, bitter." Larry took another sip. "So how about the twenty-foot cat. I haven't seen it. I figured it would just be stalking around like Godzilla."

"Oh, the cat," said Luis Grenadine Folk Jr. "She's at the vet with an infected cut on her leg. We're all pretty worried." He became misty eyed. "Knocked over a powerline and got cut."

"What's this IPA called again?" said Larry.

"Bitter Enemas," said Luis Grenadine Folk Jr. He laughed and hocked a big one.

Theme Park

Lila arrived at Theme Park ten minutes early. She was looking forward to the famous beef stew, the Ferris wheel, and a ride that goes up and down. At home, she liked to twist and tunnel through the dirty sheets on her bed. She lived in a room. Her parents had entered her name in a lottery for Theme Park tickets the day after she was born. That was thirty years ago. She stepped on a wad of cotton candy. She touched a dry cement wall and waited.

The gate opened and Lila entered. This year's theme, Brown, was in evidence. Her skirt caught in the revolving gate. She stood there. She saw a cart with roasted ears of corn. The Ferris wheel loomed in the near distance, going round and round.

A man with a fold of skin on his forehead appeared. He gripped a squeaking bundle of brown balloons.

"Hello," said Lila. She wore a box hat with a narrow chinstrap.

The balloon man wore brown. He looked uncanny. "Here you go, missy." He handed her a brown balloon.

She let it slip from her hand and it hovered, waiting. "That's a swell balloon," she said.

He saw her skirt caught in the gate. He let the balloons go, and they hovered. "May I?" He pushed the fold of skin up and down on his forehead.

Lila's heart raced. "No," she said. "You've done enough. I'll be fine." Her balloon lifted just beyond reach.

"I'm Doug," said the balloon man. "I'll be moving along."

"Goodbye, Doug," said Lila.

Lila revolved back through the gate, and it clicked to a stop. Now she couldn't reach the pinched fabric on the other side of the barrier. A line of ants marching past dispersed around her shoe, which was fragrant with cotton candy. One of the ants scurried back to the nest with news of the find.

Lila shuffled her feet. The waist of her skirt tugged. The sun burned her shoulders. "Doug?" she called out. "Doug?" An ant bit her ankle. "Doug!"

A man holding a fat beaver appeared. He followed straight brown lines drawn on the ground. He turned at a right angle to Lila and stroked the beaver, which had no teeth. "Do you need Doug?" he said.

Lila slapped an ant on her shin. "Oh," she said. "My skirt is stuck, and the ants… I'm the winner today." She looked from the ants to the man holding a beaver.

"You must be Lila Carpathian," said the man. "I'm Leo. And this is Buddy. Buddy the beaver. I see you stepped in some cotton candy and attracted the attention of ants."

"Yes, yes, I'm Lila. I'm stuck you see."

Buddy itched the beaver's ears and cleared his throat. "That guy that was here yesterday, Peter something, Peter Seagull, or maybe it was something else, he dropped his cotton candy on the way out. He left early. He didn't clean up after himself and now look what's happened."

"Oh my," said Lila. "Peter Seagull." She had dated Peter in tenth grade. He had asked her to marry him, joined the Army instead, and now this. "This is a new skirt." She brushed an ant from her knee. "Oh!"

"Here comes Doug," said Leo. "Hey, Doug. Over here." He put Buddy on the ground. Buddy waddled toward Lila.

"Oh, please," said Lila. "Shoo, shoo."

"Hi, Leo," said Doug. "What's new?"

"Lila here, today's lucky winner, stepped in some cotton candy. Peter Seagull is to blame. I knew something bad was coming when he left early. Nobody ever leaves early."

Doug released his balloons and they hovered. "What can we do?"

"Help me," said Lila.

"This is what happens," said Leo. He scratched his thigh with a key. "Buddy, leave the winner alone."

Lila shrieked and jerked away from Buddy. Her skirt ripped. She slapped ants from her legs.

"That's new," said Doug.

Lila gave a great yank and tore her skirt loose from the gate. Tears slipped down her cheeks.

"Jesus, what's next?" said Leo.

Doug watched Lila run away. He toyed with his fold of skin. "Beats me. Maybe Buddy will grow some new teeth."

They laughed, and the brown balloons lifted just beyond reach.

Charles Manson's Birthday

Regina gagged into the toilet holding to the rim like she was on a roller coaster.

"Oh Lord," said the nurse. "Did you swallow your tampon, Regina?"

Regina took a deep breath and said, "Yes." Her black hair dangled in the cold water. She wore red stretchy pants and a tight white t-shirt that said, "Kapow!" Regina wrote Charles Manson a letter each and every day. She even celebrated his birthday, November 12, 1934.

"So you're not really choking. You just swallowed it, right?" said the nurse. Her name was Nancy. Her husband called her Nancy Nurse. She wore a plain brown skirt to her ankles and a puffy tan top with a light brown jacket and an ostrich brooch.

"I just wanted you to notice me," said Regina. She flopped onto her bottom on the cold tile, hair covering her eyes.

Regina motioned for the aide Antoine to help her. Regina hiccuped. Her breath smelled like menses.

"Why you do such a thing?" said Antoine.

Nancy shook her head and grabbed Regina beneath her armpits. "Come on babydoll, let's get you into the dayroom. Dr. Bottoms will be here soon."

Regina stood and tuned to frequency 4quadrillion&8. She examined the hands under her armpits and saw them as mannequin hands. Tinny music, perhaps from France, bippity bopped inside her head. The devil was telling her to ride a bicycle to the ocean. Once there, the bicycle would float. She could pedal to Israel and see where Jesus died. She gained her balance and looked from Antoine to Nancy.

"Here we go babydoll," said Nancy. "Little baby steps to the dayroom. Here we go."

Antoine looked lost and disgusted. He had three kids. Everyday he shaved with hot water, ironed his white pants, and rode the bus to work. The nursing home did not allow perfume or cologne, but he always smelled good, like Dial soap. Regina's armpits were hot and smelled of burning steel.

Into the square dayroom they went, Regina shuffling her feet in green disposable slippers. A thin man was playing foosball by himself, spinning the rods like mad. The TV was on—*talk, talk, talk, rabble, rabble* it went.

"Yada yada yada," said Regina. She had
Charles Manson's prison ID tattooed on her
forearm, b33920. Her favorite number was
17.

"Just a few more baby steps, babydoll."

They backed her up to a mustard chair,
and Regina sat. Cattycorner to her was Wesley. He had his hand in his pants pulling his
taffy.

"Wesley, go to your room if you're going
to masturbate," said Nancy.

Wesley looked at her. He wore a red plaid
shirt and was barefoot. He liked "creamed
potatoes," not "mashed potatoes," but
"creamed potatoes." "Go to fucking hell,"
said Wesley. He kept on pulling his taffy and
then began to weep like a child.

"Oh, sweet Jesus," said Nancy. She had
to get back to her charting. "Regina, you
okay for now, babydoll?"

Regina smacked her lips and said, "Yes."

Antoine sighed and left, headed to the
bathroom to wash his hands and say a little
prayer for the world.

Clickety Clack Scatter

Even with the shunt, little Albert's head grew and grew to the size of a long watermelon. Thin, wispy, and red, his eyebrows sat a good eight inches from his eyes. Albert was perhaps the saddest creature at the nursing home, four years old, unable to lift his head. But life was not without its occasional joy. The nurse's aides at the home took fine care of Albert, turning his body every two hours, squirting baby food into the feeding tube sewn to his side, and changing his diaper at least once per shift.

Albert's favorite nurse's aide was Debbie Dee. She often had cold sores, but no matter. She fussed over Albert, put baby powder on his privates, and would hold her index finger in his rectum when he became constipated. Albert was just one of the bunch.

One thing Albert could do and do well was suck. Debbie Dee kept a big round sucker in his mouth and as a result he drooled and his teeth rotted into scraps of brown and black. Debbie Dee knew there was trouble when Albert refused the sucker and cried

with pain, darting his thick tongue in and
out. It was his teeth, and he needed to go
to the dentist, not easy considering Albert's
giant head and his flaccid neck. Dr. Hallway
Jr. approved and the trip was on, set for a
Saturday morning.

Albert did just fine in the back of the brown
A-OK cab, strapped in double, one for his
waist and one for his head. The strap rubbed
a burn on his cheek, but what could be
done? Debbie Dee rode up front, her bosom
divided by the seat strap, her little paper
nurse's hat clipped with Bobby pins. She
smelled chili and cigarettes, not a bad combination. The taxi meter shone bright red,
flipping in ten-cent increments.

It took Debbie Dee, the taxi driver, *and*
the dentist to carry Albert like a long sack of
potatoes into the office. Dr. Brownbrick laid
the chair flat so that Albert's extensive head
would not hang off the back. Dr. Brownbrick glanced at his clean fingers, smelling
of soap, and the plastic tray covered with
pointy instruments. Time to get to work. No
use delaying matters. The nursing home was
a freak show at times, but a goldmine nonetheless.

"Albert, precious baby, Debbie Dee's
right here, holding your little hand, sweet-

heart. Lord, look at your teeth!"

Dr. Brownbrick wedged in a mouthpiece to keep Albert's mouth open. A rank air of digested baby food wafted from Albert's mouth. "Hmm," said Dr. Brownbrick. He decided right away that he was going to pull all twenty teeth, maybe cut out a couple, just ragged stumps of stained ivory. He wasn't licensed to cut out teeth, but there were seven days in the week and he intended to make the most of them all. He turned on some Ferlin Husky to get in a tooth-pulling mood.

"Can you tell little Albert here that I'm going to pull his teeth out, real slow, one at a time?" said Dr. Brownbrick. He checked his Movado watch, his wife's, but it kept the time.

"Dear Jesus," said Debbie Dee. "Albert, babydoll, honey, we're gonna get those nasty teeth out for you, honey, then you can suck on suckers all day long. Yum, yum, yummy yum." She licked her lips for Albert's benefit and ran her hand across his enormous elongated head. Goosebumps washed across Albert's neck. She reached down and picked up a can of hairspray. Beneath the logo "HairSet 5000," she read this: "Until you learn to work the microwave, don't expect to get ahead. Go the extra mile and familiarize yourself with Google Earth as well and then some doors are bound to open."

"Damn hairspray," said Dr. Brownbrick. It had been a hairspray can that had recommended he be circumcised as an adult.

"You gonna numb him up good, doctor?" said Debbie Dee.

"He won't know the difference," said the doctor. "Plus he might have an allergic reaction." The tooth extractor went in and grabbed a baby molar. The tooth plugged out with a slushy sound and blood began to pool. "Here, suck the blood for me." He jammed the suction wand into Debbie Dee's good hand.

"Yessir," said Debbie Dee. She looked around for a diploma on the wall and didn't see one. Albert was moaning now, his cry of pain, the moan he used when tape got in his pubic hair or his pee ran hot. "Sweet precious baby," said Debbie Dee.

Out came another tooth, roots dripping blood and pus. Albert's moan went high pitched and his fat chin quivered. He tried to raise his hands to his mouth but he couldn't make them work. *Clink!* went the tooth in a porcelain tray. *Suck suck!* went the suction wand, whisking away ropes of blood and saliva.

"Dear blessed child." Debbie Dee stroked

the length of his head.

The next tooth, a canine, slid out with relative ease trailing behind it a tangled gray cord of nerve. That made Dr. Brownbrick wince and regret that he had not become a mortician as his father had suggested. He gave it a little tug and the nerve snapped like an earthworm.

"Dumpling, sweet dumpling." Debbie Dee could barely keep up with the suction wand. She glanced at her engagement ring, $99 on sale, but it was better than nothing.

Dr. Brownbrick stifled a gag and out came another tooth. The dish was filling quickly. One tooth snapped in half, but those things happened. He couldn't wait to get in the hot tub at the YMCA. All those bubbles! and he knocked the bowl of teeth into the floor, *clickety clack scatter!*

Renewal

Pete worked at the yellow court house. His code name was Clozar, but only to his close friend(s). He was thin in the arms but had a paunch. He cut his own hair.

The day was like any other day. It had begun and would end. Bleach was on sale at the Food Kingdom. He would stop by after work and take a case. You just never knew.

Issuing license plates was not necessarily "fun," but it did pay the bills. Pete examined the line curving around the see-through partition and into the hall. The man who was next approached, towering over Pete.

"Lean forward so that I can inject your head with bleach," said Pete.

"What?" said the man. He held a checkbook.

"I said, license and registration please." Pete frowned. No one had a sense of humor any more. The transaction complete, Pete waited for the next "customer." He scratched his head down the part in his hair.

"I need to report a stolen license plate," said the new customer, a woman with red hair and red lipstick.

"Well, to get us started, you'll need to bend over and take a huge bleach enema," said Pete. "Don't worry. It was on sale."

"I see," said the woman. Her name was Doris and she was in the dry cleaning business. "And then do I need to drink a formaldehyde milkshake and do the Hokey Pokey?"

Pete's face brightened. "You do shirts for three bucks."

"I do indeed," said Doris. She winked at Pete.

"Well first you'll need to bend over," said Pete. He hefted a gallon jug of bleach from beneath his desk.

The Day Before School Starts

The day before school started, August 25, Mrs. Hodges tried to pull Scarlet from the baby pool, where she had been all summer. The water had evaporated and Scarlet's waste had glued her in place. She was limp, lethargic, and sunburned a deep red-bronze.

It took a paint scraper and a gallon of distilled water to loosen Scarlet from the plastic pool. Mrs. Hodges decided to let Scarlet soak in the pool overnight. She got the hose and some green dishwashing detergent. Scarlet floated in the water with a smile, picking the detritus from her skin.

"Here you go, babydoll," said her mother. She emptied a bread bag full of crusts—she didn't feed those to the ducks—into a floating bowl for Scarlet. She tipped on a few drops of hot sauce for variety. "Now don't mess in the pool tonight, hear? Tomorrow's school and we got to get you looking pretty." She dumped in a cup of Clorox and dropped in a can of hairspray.

Charlotte grabbed the can and read this:

"Tonight, a wolf will visit. He will keep you warm." Charlotte's eyes grew wide with excitement. A wolf!

A gibbous moon slashed a silver of light in the night sky. A freak cold front roared into Pianotown and it began to snow. Charlotte shivered in the water, covered with wet flakes. From the hairspray can she had fashioned a crude but sharp knife and waited, flailing her arms for warmth.

The light went out in her mother's bedroom window. The wind howled and sleet burned Charlotte's face. She was excited about school. According to another hairspray can, third grade would be a "banner year" filled with "high hopes."

A hungry wolf trotted into the snowy gale, nose to the ground, ears pinned back. Its fur was as thick as a bear's. It was hungry. Up Charlotte's street it came, pausing at a grapefruit peel soaked in milk. It licked the freezing rind and moved on. Its eyes saw the little human in the pool before its scent arrived. The wolf's shoulder blades slunk into points as it tiptoed toward the baby pool. Saliva cloyed its mouth, and it stifled a sneeze.

A skim of ice had formed. The cold wracked Charlotte's body. The wind

whipped and howled. Only the freezing
water kept the pool from flying away. Then,
like a mouse, Charlotte became still, her
breathing shallow. Fangs dug into the back
of her neck and blood oozed like oil from the
punctures.

Charlotte reached back and with her
thumb blinded the wolf in one eye. The wolf
released her and Charlotte grabbed its neck,
the knife in her hand. The wolf reared like a
horse, fell on the knife, and rolled over top
heavy. It snapped at the air just below its
chin. Charlotte was thrilled to be embracing
a real wolf. She grabbed its neck with one
hand and slid the blade between its ribs,
puncturing the heart. The wolf staggered
and fell on top of Charlotte, and there she
slept through the night kept warm by the
furry corpse.

Love Lifted Me

Simon parked his mom's F150 on the shoulder of the bridge. The interstate ran beneath. He undressed and squatted to pee one last time. The sun was at his back, no doubt in the eyes of the drivers headed west. It was easy to climb over and jump. The voices were finally with him, and he dropped like a stone.

~

Where Simon's tattoo of a dragon had been on his left breast, there was a mess of serous fluid and blood. Simon lay poolside on the hard cement, propped on his elbows, wearing black shades. He'd grown weary of the tattoo and burned it off with a pack of cigarettes, his mom's Virginia Slims. Simon looked up when his brother-in-law Nate walked into the pool with the two little ones. Simon had an erection and pulled his knees up higher to hide it. The voices were raging, telling him to jack off, to *pull it out, pull it out, pull it out…* He was exhausted but composed. The splashing and children yelling were doing a weird music making him feel that he was undulating. He pressed his palms to the hot cement.

"Simon, what the hell happened?" said Nate. He glanced back at his son and daughter, hovering by the shallow end of the pool. They knew some things about Uncle Simon.

Simon kept an even keel. "Well, what happened to you?" His face remained blank.

"Oh, Lord," said Nate. He knew it was hopeless to ask Simon questions. Simon just turned them around. He'd have to tell his wife, Simon's sister, and that would ruin the day once that happened. "Are you okay, man?"

"Are you okay?" said Simon. His hands were on fire. Sounds were coming at him through metal pipes… *beat it, beat it, beat it, you motherfucker, beat it…*

"Okay, okay," said Nate. He turned away.

~

Simon lived with his mother. He would not take his medication and his mother let him slide. He was her baby after all. She was hopeful when Simon started delivering the *Pianotown Register* to mailboxes, but he quit after a week.

While his mother was at church, Simon masturbated. He came once but then it was hopeless. He kept on, driven by the voices telling him to die. He turned on the shopping channel and watched a young woman modeling a red sundress. *Die motherfucker, die,* said the voices. He tried harder, sweating, beating and beating himself to a pulp. The voices went tinny and faster. His hand was tired. His back was tired. Every light in the house was on. His bedroom was a wreck. He looked in the fridge and saw lemonade and barbecue sauce. He had a sudden urge to see himself in the mirror. Maybe it wasn't true. Maybe it wasn't him. Maybe he was somebody else and this was all a huge fucking mistake. The scab was soggy on his chest. He took a nail file and poked it. *Die motherfucker die.*

At church, Bettyanne, Simon's mother sang along with the choir, *Love Lifted Me. When nothing else could help, love lifted me...* She thought about him the entire time. She remembered when he was five and used to wear a cute black hat to church.

Simon saw a tiny glimmer of hope. He turned the shopping channel up full volume to drown the voices. He would just have to help himself, just like he had with the tattoo. He turned on the radio too, classic rock,

"Godzilla" by Blue Oyster Cult, wide open.
The solution was solidifying in his head, in
his hand.

Bettyanne felt a thrill of panic thread
through her chest. She should not have left
him alone. She said a prayer for Simon, that
he would find peace on this Earth.

Simon called 911 before he did it. "I need
an ambulance," he told the dispatcher. "Any
particular reason?" "There's just gonna be
a lot of blood and I'll need an ambulance."
The noise of the radio and TV felt good. He
was feeling a kind of peace.

Bettyanne hurried to the choir room and
hung up her robe. She had to get home and
quick.

Simon took off his clothes and stepped
up to the kitchen table. It was the right
height. His penis was red and shriveled. He
stretched it and with a bread knife began to
saw through the shaft. He stopped to catch
his breath and continued. The last bit took
some effort, but it was done.

Bettyanne ran a stop sign.

He took a butcher knife and filleted what he
had removed. He held a towel over the gush-
ing stump and waited. From now on, until
he jumped from the bridge, he would have
to squat to pee.

What God Looks Like

There were three things Silas wanted from life. He wanted to love someone. He wanted to be loved. He wanted to meet God *before* he died.

Silas pulled out of Pianotown headed cross-country to Truckee, California, with a load of used whiskey barrels. The barrels had been cut in half and stacked—58,000 pounds of whiskey barrels, 29,000 pounds per axle, 2,227 miles one way. He would spend the night in Kearney, Nebraska.

Right around Platte City, Kansas, Silas passed a hitchhiker wearing a yellow suit of some sort. Looked like a jogging outfit. The sun was high and headed west, blue skies smeared with marshmallow fluff. He hit his turn signal, downshifted and braked, pulling onto the median. Gravel flew and zinged. He brought the rig to a dead stop and waited.

It took the hitchhiker a minute to catch up. He was waving, using a walking stick, and carrying a beat-up frame pack. Silas watched him approach and a tingle ran from his belly button to just below his chin. He shifted his buttocks, sore from the ride. The cab smelled like farts and coffee.

Daniel climbed up like a pro and hopped in, swinging his pack like a sack of potatoes. He was a poet, on his way to Portland, and had about half a bachelor's degree in history under his belt. The first thing Silas noticed was that Daniel's face seemed to be that of a girl, smooth and soft, delicate cheekbones, hair curled around his ears. He felt a tug on his heart.

"Do you love me?" said Silas.

Daniel, always the poet, said, "I love you as much as you love me, I suppose. Headed west?"

Silas nodded, realizing that two of his wishes in life were being fulfilled. "How does one meet God before one dies? Do you know?" said Silas

Daniel pulled a snack cracker from his pack and opened it. He wanted to eat it with some Vienna sausage, wash it down with diet root beer. "Hmm, I suppose that God requires a great sacrifice, and then he will come down in His glory and say Hello or something like that. Does that work?"

Silas thought of Abraham and his son Isaac. "That makes sense," he said. He eased back in his seat, wondering how best to cut Daniel's throat.

Cold Sores and Meteorites

After the liquid concentrate is fed into the can and the propellant is injected, followed by the sealing of the can, the cans of pressurized hairspray pass into a trough of hot water. This is where Henry sits on a barstool eight and a half hours a day looking for trails of tiny bubbles that indicate a leaking can. Henry is quiet, in the habit of adopting stray dogs, and a pretty good bowler. He minds his own business and is shy around women.

Henry stops outside the hairspray factory, tugs on his brown corduroy pants, and steps into the phone booth there. The phone is off the hook and squawking so he replaces it in the cradle. He checks the can of hairspray there and reads this: "Don't let cold sores prevent you from looking for a girlfriend. You don't get cold sores as much as you used to, plus you could grow a beard, which would hide the scabs. Watch out, though, for meteorites."

He chuckles and walks east down Main

Street past the yellow court house. A meteorite streaks across the horizon, crashes through the court house, and hits him in the groin. He falls to the ground, moaning and confused. Beneath the surface, the femoral artery springs a leak and bleeds into the skin. It looks like a purple football growing there. The pressure is unbearable, and he faints.

Henry makes the *Pianotown Register,* the front page. Apparently the only other person to have been hit by a meteorite is a woman from Sylacauga, Alabama. He awakes in the "intensive care unit," really just a three-bed outfit in the nursing home with piped oxygen and suction in the walls. He feels the sharp pain in his groin, where a sandbag has been applied with a tight, elastic bandage.

The nurse enters and she is really pretty, slim with curvy hips and a firm bust. Her name is Dolores and she likes dogs. She's very outgoing but prefers quiet men.

Henry smiles at Dolores and feels cold sores swelling the corners of his mouth. It's too late to grow a beard and his heart sinks.

Allergic to Water

Tall with rusty hair, Rachel stepped in cat feces and cursed. Then she realized it wasn't feces but cat vomit, and she felt a tiny bit better. Outside, the day was blue, but inside the world felt cramped and gray. She wore the same faded pants suit as yesterday. It was bad enough to carry around alien DNA, but she had transferred that DNA to her daughter Clorette. Clorette looked as human as other little girls but she was allergic to water. Tears made her eyes swell shut. A quick shower caused the skin on her chest to go lumpy, redden, and her breathing to become ragged. Just a sip of water was agony and it was all that Rachel could do to keep Clorette from turning to stone. And now she had stepped in cat vomit!

There were plenty of planets in the universe where there was little or no water, obvious homes to the aliens who had visited Earth and procreated with humans. When her husband had found out, he had left in a hurry, leaving Rachel and Clorette to fend for themselves.

Rachel figured the cat had a hairball that would either not pass through or come up. She found the hairball medicine, a thick salve of fish liver oil, put a dollop on her finger and blew on the cat's face. The pink mouth opened and in went her finger.

"Ah!" The cat bit her.

Rachel gathered her keys and purse, headed to the emergency room. Already her finger was red and swelling.

She supposed that the aliens could have come from Mars. There was no water there, but there also seemed to be no signs of life. Doctors had diagnosed her daughter Clorette with aquagenic urticaria, but had not mapped her DNA, much to Rachel's relief. She sometimes suspected that the doctors knew about the alien DNA, but that they were trained to keep quiet.

Once in the car, the smell was overpowering. It was cat feces after all that she had stepped in and not cat vomit. She rolled the window down, favoring her finger. A red streak extended across the back of her hand. The gas tank was on empty, and she gave a little shriek.

There were plenty of crazy human diseases and deformities that could be attributed to aliens, fibrous dysplasia for example or hypohidrotic ectodermal dysplasia, both conditions making their "victims" look like freaks or rather "aliens."

A yellow school bus ran a red light and plowed into the passenger side door of Rachel's old pickup. The truck was all she could afford on her salary at the hairspray factory, and her husband was behind in child support. Clorette, their daughter, wasn't even a "child" he had argued; she was an "alien."

Rachel wound up in the emergency room, unconscious, bleeding from the side of her head and suffering a dislocated shoulder. As she regained awareness, her first thought was for her daughter. She tried to sit up but fell back in pain.

"Hold on baby," said the nurse. "You're in the hospital. You were in an accident."

"My daughter," said Rachel.

"Your daughter?" said the nurse

Rachel's head swam. "Clorette, my daughter. She suffers from aquagenic urticaria. She's allergic to water. She has alien DNA and I have to pick her up at school at three. Oh, my god."

"Alright babydoll. Maybe her daddy can pick her up? I can make some phone calls for you, honey."

"No, he left because of the alien DNA." Rachel gripped the rails of the stretcher, nausea building in her throat.

The nurse stepped beyond the curtain to speak with the physician, Dr. Serat. "She's talking about aliens and DNA. Something about her daughter."

The doctor frowned. "Did she say that her daughter was allergic to water?"

"She did."

"I'll need to speak with the patient alone," said Dr. Serat. "Her EKG looks bad. Looks like she had some chest trauma, cardiac contusions. I wouldn't be surprised if she suddenly converted to a fatal arrhythmia."

Rachel clutched the sheet. She smelled cat feces, and there was something familiar about the doctor's eyes.

The Red Wagon

Alicia, the bartender, enjoyed hearing snatches of conversation as she orbited behind the particleboard bar covered in oak veneer.

"I fry mine in butter…"

"I want *her* to sit on my face…"

"Smell my finger…"

"Pianotown sucks…"

"Reverend Magpie fluttered his tongue…"

She was a good sport, looked for the best in people, and wasn't bad looking either. In fact, most of the patrons came to be mesmerized by her petite figure, her short blonde hair that looked plastic, and that wicked half smile. Men, women, and in between. She dropped a few brews in a sink full of ice.

"So you duct-tape them to a mechanic's creeper, those flat trolley things, and they move back and forth on a wire that passes through their gut?" said Tony. His oily perm jiggled.

"That's right," said James (Dr. Hartman).

"I'm getting ready to race Eddie and Pearl."
He sniffed his ale, which smelled like freshly
washed genitals.

"There's a couple of folks named Eddie
and Pearl who are missing," said Tony.

"Well, they're in my basement, duct-
taped to mechanic's creepers."

Alicia tucked a dishtowel in her back
pocket and moved to the other side of the
bar where Father McGlawn was holding
confessional across from the bourbon and
Scotch.

"It's all my fault that the wolf bit her,"
said a woman with a belly that stretched her
turquoise knit pants into a globe. Her bellybutton was Sri Lanka. "I didn't know it was
going to snow. The wolves come to town
when it snows."

Father McGlawn stirred his bourbon with
a red toothpick. "Well, she's alive."

"But, those holes in the back of her
neck."

Alicia wiped the counter and tapped the
tip jar with a pencil for good luck. She took
a few steps sideways to catch a conversation
between Nancy, a nurse who worked at the
nursing home and an old high school chum,
Tonya Sitzbath. Alicia polished a glass with
her dishtowel.

"She swallows tampons?" said Tonya.

She had lost her child recently in a tornado, sucked right from her arms.

"You bet your diddly squat she does," said Nancy. She threw back the tequila, no lime no salt, and wiped her mouth.

"Do they, do they pass through?"

"Is the sun really just a big yellow nuclear oven?" said Nancy.

Alicia poured another tequila for Nancy and walked over to the trivia machine where A.E. Baker Dearborn Jr. sat thrumming his fingers and staring at the screen.

"Got any new beheading videos?" said Alicia.

A.E. Baker Dearborn Jr. ignored her for a moment. He wore a plaid coat. He was getting bored with beheading videos. "Got one from Albania, kidnapping gone bad. It's on YouTube." He yawned.

Conversation, alcohol. She checked out the English professor, the one with the little scab on top of his head. His glasses made him look sexy. Alicia yawned.

The Star Spangled Banner

Before Darla Scoren "abused" her adopted
son from Russia, the husky child Leonard,
she liked to kill one of his pets. Thus, the
long string of dogs, cats, and hamsters that
came and went at 3 Beanfellow Lane.

Little boys were evil creatures to Darla,
good for yard work only. So, until Leonard
was old enough to push a lawnmower, he
was essentially useless, a curiosity.

Darla was tall with a pointy chin. A few
stiff hairs grew there, which she kept in
check with tweezers. She had large oval eyes
that seemed ready to weep. She was not
buxom, but had long breasts like hanging
bananas. She was always "fixin" to do something, "fixin to eat" or "fixin to go to the
store."

She had adopted Leonard when he was
only nine months old. She'd been married
at the time, working as an accountant at the
hairspray factory. It was her husband who
started the "abuse," and now she blamed
little Leonard for the whole thing, divorce,

lost job, and all.

Leonard was a dear child, portly, a big eater of sweets, withdrawn, and a lover of animals. He was shy around other children and carried a little piece of his baby blanket in his pocket, which he pulled out and smelled when he was nervous or upset.

It was Friday and Darla had an hour between her shift at the car wash and her shift at the Corn Dog Palace. She stormed into Leonard's room. He ran to the corner and hid his face. After Darla strangled his new baby rat with her thumb and forefinger, she slapped his face several times until his nose bled. He said not a word.

Then she pulled the toy piano from the closet and Leonard began to whimper. It was time for an ice water enema and the "Star Spangled Banner."

The Corn Dog Palace smelled like grease and more grease. Each frozen corndog was dropped in a deep fryer for one minute and forty seconds, then lifted out with a basket to let the oil *drip, drip, drip*.

"May I take your order?" said Darla. It was the woman, Doreen, who lived in the giant litter box with the giant cat. Apparently she was getting ready to move into a giant coffee can.

"Yes," said Doreen. "I found this can of

hairspray in my yard and on the side I read this: "A woman named Darla at the Corndog Palace gives her adopted son ice water enemas, and he has to hold them while she plays the "Star Spangled Banner" on a toy piano. If you tell her that you know about the enemas, she's liable to give you a free corndog."

Darla smirked down her long nose at Doreen, who wore a white dress with a white sash. "Would you like the special?"

"Yes, I would," said Doreen. The giant coffee can had arrived last week, and she was waiting on the mustachioed man and their one night of love together. Apparently, he was riding a bus from El Salvador and had been delayed by bad weather in Texas.

Darla rang up a special—two corndogs, a tall fruit punch, and a battered deep fried vanilla Twinkie, the generic kind. She lost control of her bowels and the remainder of the ice water enema gushed into her pants. "That'll be four eighty-nine," said Darla.

"There must be some mistake," said Doreen.

"Yes," said Darla. "There is. I kill one of his pets, and then *I* take the ice water enema, not *him*."

"Oh," said Doreen, reaching for her purse.

You Must Be Born Again

Evelyn moved with the contraction, her body swimming sideways and forward. Each end of the mahogany sleigh bed on which she lay was stacked with pillows. The plastic shower curtain beneath her glued itself to the small of her back. Evelyn processed claims for Medicaid patients and was in the habit of giving away money to her clients. Sweat clung to her fuzzed upper lip. She was neither large nor small, the size of a healthy mannequin, proportioned to insinuate a medium build. A forelock of blonde hair formed a question mark on her forehead. The room smelled of stress, *sturm und drang*, the struggle of fin, fur, and feather against barbed hooks, steel traps, and lead shot.

In the driveway of the 1930's two-bedroom bungalow was the doula's small bronze economy car with Tennessee license plates. The trunk was filled with Brazilian birthing videos, aquamarine suction bulbs, cat litter, and a case of yellow Gatorade.

In the backyard, a series of three small

goldfish ponds burbled, their flow powered by a black sump pump in the lowest pond. Wisteria vines bulged through the boards of the privacy fence, warping the planks. In the distance was visible the cupola of the town's yellow court house.

Across from Evelyn lay Betsy, propped against the footboard, droopy, fidgeting with the seams of her thin gown. Her feet touched Evelyn's feet. As Evelyn arched, so did she. It had been twenty-eight days since Betsy birthed her eleventh child, a twelve-pound boy named Eric. Betsy was larger than Evelyn, wider in the hips, and topped with a mat of short graying black hair. She liked to bowl and could hook the ball with her left hand. Her kids pretty much looked after themselves, so league nights were not a problem. Betsy panted with Evelyn, in sync with her struggle.

"Two hours have passed," the doula said, "since the onset of labor." The doula was slim with a paunch, like she was holding a purse beneath her bellybutton. Evelyn was at eight centimeters and struggling not to push just yet. She bellowed as the con-tractions gripped her and the baby shifted, dropping lower, pressing against her bladder and spine.

"Oh God," said Evelyn.

The doula wiped sweat from Evelyn's forehead. "Getting ready to push. Take another sip of Gatorade." She tilted the plastic bottle to Evelyn's lips.

Evelyn groaned and nodded, a quick smile. She could feel her heart beating in her lips. Her water had broken over an hour ago. It was time. She was fed up with religion and had decided to take matters into her own hands. Her husband, "the preacher," had run off with the part-time secretary who routinely screwed up the Sunday bulletins. On one occasion, she had misspelled sacred as scared.

"Thank you," said Evelyn.

"You're welcome," said the doula. "Ready to push?" She pulled her gloved hand from Evelyn's vagina.

Outside, a mockingbird teased a stray cat, swooping in big Us (ewes). The cat flipped on its back and nearly caught the bird. In the west, the sun hung at three o'clock as if stuck in the sky. To the east, a faint outline of the moon.

"Oh sweet Jesus!" said Evelyn. She wanted to say goddamn, but just couldn't.

"Breathe in, breath out! Push!" said the doula.

Evelyn rose up against the pillows and bore down. She felt as if she were having a large bowel movement. She exhaled a tremendous moan. Her breasts seemed about to burst.

"Don't hold your breath, Evelyn. Breathe in, breathe out," said the doula.

Betsy looked at her hands, waiting.

"One more cigarette," said the doula. "Just keep pushing."

"Okay," said Evelyn.

Outside, the doula lit up and streamed white smoke through her pinched lips. She saw a can of hairspray on the hood of her bronze car, let her cigarette-hand go limp, and stepped down from the battleship-gray porch. Beside the silhouette of a woman's hairdo she read: "Whatever you do, don't kink the umbilical cord and don't clear the baby's lungs. You should have just enough time before the placenta begins to separate and blood flow ceases to the fetus." She nodded. She smelled meat drying in the sun.

Evelyn reminded the doula of a cement truck churning its heavy load. "Push! I can see the crown! Ooh, a head full of black hair." The doula reached over and squeezed Betsy's hand. "Get ready. Soon, now, soon."

Betsy's eyes grew dim with reality. She pressed her feet against Evelyn's. Evelyn shook and trembled, forcing out each breath with a purple face. It seemed as if her eyes would leave the sockets. The doula was wrestling with the baby now. It was turning, face down, shoulders slipping through the stretched muscles and tissue. The hair, the skin covered in a film of cheesy vernix. It's little chin quivering, eyes clamped shut. Purple.

"Jesus, Mary, Mother of God!" said Evelyn. She felt the baby slide from her loins, gasped, and fell back against the pillows.

The doula wrested the baby free, squirting its head with a thick rope of lubricating jelly, smearing it quickly over the shoulders.

Betsy thought about how expensive groceries were, spread her legs, and groaned.

Trapping

Stephen checked his traps every two days. He didn't need a snowmobile, but he used one anyway. He pulled into the parking lot of the Pianotown Library and roared up beside the green outdoor book return. The gaping jaws of his spring trap were empty but the snatch of caribou fur he used for bait was still there. He tipped his dog fur cap to a toddler and went inside to see if the latest copy of *Snafu Magazine* had arrived.

"Hi, Carol," said Stephen. He held up his hand with fingers extended, palm facing her.

Carol wore metal hair rollers to work. "Hi, Stephen." She resumed helping an elderly woman search for recipes that called for seedless raisins.

Stephen moved on, making eye contact with a staunch lesbian and then a little boy with white tennis shoes. Money was tight, traps were empty, and until the people stopped feeding the beavers and such, his hopes to clear the year without a loss were spare.

"Say Stephen, how are things?" It was

Father McGlawn. His mouth bore likeness to an ovoid tunnel.

Stephen pushed his snow goggles back, bunching his thick gray hair. "Well, hello." He squirmed inside his down vest, sweat running between his breasts, branching along a swatch of hair to his waist.

"Haven't seen you at mass lately."

Stephen thought of the endless nights spent at truck stop strip joints, the jeering at his snowmobile, how none of the ladies took him seriously. "Well, my mother has been ill, you know, with Chagas disease." The library lights hummed along, reminding him of the church choir.

"Oh, the flagellate protozoan *Trypanosoma cruzi*. Transmitted by kissing bugs. Any idea how she came into contact with the vector?"

"Probably from digging wells in Guatemala when she was young and care free," said Stephen.

Father McGlawn texted himself a message to put Stephen's mother on the prayer list. "Well, I'm putting it in high gear. See you soon and tell your mother *Buenos dias*."

Stephen pursed his lips, nodded, and headed to the periodicals, swinging his dog fur cap by its black strap.

Rasputin

The man who emerged from the phone booth in front of the hairspray factory was Rasputin. He wore a long brown robe and damp leather slippers. His limp brown hair framed a sharp face, the hair draping down to blend with his ample beard. His dark eyes were round and piercing. He reached down for a can of hairspray. In addition to "manly fragrance" and "super holding power" (in Russian) he read this: "The mayor believes in ghosts and will find your connections to the spirit world of utmost interest."

Rasputin clicked his tongue, thirsty for wine and the company of learned women, and he stepped across the street to the yellow court house, which was also City Hall.

"May I serve you," said the receptionist. She had bright red hair and wasn't wearing underwear. She liked to open and close her legs beneath her desk, feeling the suck of warm air out and the rush of cool air in.

Speaking only Russian and a little French, Rasputin drew pictures in the air with his bony fingers.

"You want to climb the flagpole?" said the receptionist. She wore a blouse with blue triangles on it. "You want to fly like a bird?"

Rasputin shook his head No and continued. After fifteen minutes or so, the receptionist got it. "Oh, you want to see the mayor. You are a mystic visiting from beyond the grave. I see. And you want to weasel your way into the mayor's inner circle where you will lay traps and build power for yourself. I see."

Rasputin nodded and smiled at the receptionist, fingering the brass cross about his neck. She was dispensable, a minor character in his play. He thought about strangling her, making love to her. He resisted the urge to brush a bit of fuzz from her shoulder.

The receptionist dialed the mayor's phone. "Yes, there is a Russian mystic here to see you. Mm hm. Yes sir." She stood and ushered Rasputin through an archway across thick blue carpet. She pointed across the cavernous room, and there was the mayor waving his short arm, a watch strangling his fat wrist.

Inside the mayor's office, Rasputin admired the leather-bound books, the shiny desk, and the drapes. Floor to ceiling and as thick as a rabbit's foot! But, there was no samovar.

Mayor Riesling adjusted the flexible band of his watch and motioned for Rasputin to sit. He explained in slow English just what he needed—that Rasputin could cure his wife's anxiety, that Rasputin could resurrect his daughter's pet iguana that had died of a sudden (choked on cauliflower), that Rasputin could put a spell on his arch enemy, the principal of Pianotown High School, and that Rasputin could enlarge the width of his penis.

Rasputin, without fail, granted the desires of Mayor Riesling. In the process, he slept with Riesling's wife Marcia, defiled his son, murdered his dogs, drank up most of his wine cellar, and smoked his Cuban cigars.

A great uproar ensued against Rasputin. The Police Chief, Harold, despised Rasputin's influence over City Hall. Because of Rasputin, the mayor had closed the city jail, releasing the inmates. One, a half-wit named Bobby, had been killed walking across the interstate. Another promptly began exposing his underdeveloped genitals at the library. It was worse than an outbreak of cicadas.

Hearing of Rasputin's plans to close the high school, Principal Fixate rallied the troops, luring Rasputin to the home of high school cheerleader Amanda Pfister, whose father ran the local National Guard Armory. Once there, Rasputin was served a rhubarb pie laced with cyanide, which had no effect on him. Amanda produced a scimitar from Yemen and slashed open his belly, the guts falling into Rasputin's hands. Babbling in Russian, Rasputin took a bullet in the forehead, fired by an English spy.

Still alive, Rasputin stumbled through the kitchen door onto the back deck. Grabbed from behind by a cadre of ROTC students, Rasputin plunged headfirst into a waiting hot tub where he took in a long draught of water, filling his lungs. Finished, Rasputin ascended to Heaven, or Hell, depending on which can of hairspray you believe.

Aliens in Haiti

Dressed in a gray sweatsuit, a ballcap that advertised the bank he was robbing, and sunglasses, Danny Gillespie shot little Jordan Adams in the head with a rickety .22 pistol. He walked from the bank, ran around to the back, jumped in a white pickup and fled the scene. No one saw his escape, too focused on the dying child.

~

Jordan was a curious little two-year-old boy. He ate marshmallows for breakfast and possessed alien DNA. His mother, a single mom who worked in the coffee shop, Creamy Black, took him to work with her. She kept him in a small backroom filled with bags of green coffee beans and boxes of coffee cups.

He played well by himself, climbing the bags of beans, making up cup games, singing, and deciphering coded messages from alien headquarters in Port-au-Prince, Haiti. Jordan knew much more than he had the ability to speak. He knew about the big earthquake that devastated the south of Haiti in 2010, knew about it before it happened, knew that the United States government had set off a small nuclear device in the Gulf of Mexico, which triggered the earthquake that killed over 200,000 people. The feds were out to uncover alien operations on Earth, to destroy them if possible, and he knew that the terrible poverty in Haiti was merely a curtain, a disguise to cover the aliens' presence.

Danny Gillespie, a former British spy, followed Jordan and his mother as they walked to the bank. The robbery would be a cover to further rid the Earth of alien influence. Danny lived in Vancouver and had been staying at the Pianotown Motor Lodge, registered under the name, Carlotti de Franco. Danny was not handsome nor was he plain. His nose was rather sharp, his eyes a furious brown. The day was sunny, warm, and he walked past the little girl named Scarlet who spent her summers in a baby pool. He smelled meat drying in the sun.

Inside the bank, he removed his shades and hat to make himself less suspicious. He wore a fake black beard and had a fake tattoo of a horse on his forearm. The line was rather long and he waited patiently, just two customers ahead of Jordan and his mom.

At the counter, Carlotti de Franco, *aka* Danny Gillespie, poked his gun from beneath his sweat shirt and told the teller to empty her drawer into a money pouch and hand it over "pronto," although he actually said "proton," which confused the teller, a young lady who believed in luck and astrology.

Money in hand, Danny turned to finish his business.

Jordan's mother screamed.

A Yearning, an Earning

Gripping her "meat curtains," Vivian LaRouche exposed her birth canal. She sat, legs spread, in a plastic folding chair, wearing a bikini top the color of birds' eggs.

~

Vivian's following consisted of men with shaved heads, usually single men in their twenties. The whole affair had begun years earlier with the birth of her first child, a girl she named Caprice. During labor, as she pushed with all her might, little Caprice's head had appeared then withdrawn, pushed out a bit and then slipped back again. It was an overwhelming sensation, a powerful dirge within her groin that she did not experience with her subsequent eight births.

Vivian's last child was born dead, the cord wrapped three times around its neck. She entered a period of postpartum depression and soul searching. That powerful urge to have a skull slide back and forth in her vaginal canal, to breach the inner labia and then pull back, push forward and slide back, returned full force. She longed for that ache.

Standing a bit over five feet, Vivian liked to wear soft, worn jeans with bright tops. She liked the way the jeans gripped her tummy and made it flat. Her eyes, dark brown and wide with wonder, were her singular feature. Vivian was a good mother, a good wife to her husband, who sold infant formula in bulk, and talented as well. She'd had the lead all those years ago in her high school's rendition of "Pianotown Unfolds!" and she could tell great stories, especially bedtime stories.

A few years later, when her husband crossed the River Jordan at the age of 52, she had an epiphany. In addition to getting a job to support the three children remaining at home, she had to rediscover the joy of giving birth, stopping the birth, pulling it back in, pushing it back out, that godlike grip over life and death.

~

She stared at the young man applying lubricant to his shaved head, tucked the twenty into her bikini strap, and motioned for him to come inside.

Bedbugs

Debbie Dee sits at her vanity, rubbing lotion onto her shoulders and knees. Her blonde hair is short and clean. She's wearing a bra and faded panties with purple flowers. She hears a scruffy rustling, a scurrying across wood floors, and turns as the bedroom door pushes open.

~

Jeremy scratched his jawline. He felt itchy bumps. He threw back the sheet and noticed his legs covered with red welts, too large to be mosquito bites, perhaps two dozen in all. The sores appeared red and violent, as if probed by a dull, filthy needle or jabbed with a sharp toothpick. He stumbled upon standing, the room rounding at the edges of his vision. He was too old to sack groceries, but he did anyway.

He examined the welts on his chin in the mirror. His thin brown hair grew on top in the shape of a horseshoe. His hair was too long, and it kinked when he slept, thus the ballcaps. His favorite ballcap read, "Holy

Toledo!" He wore the hat religiously, except when he couldn't find it among the piles of dirty jeans, t-shirts, or towels. He'd found an old queen-size mattress at the dead end, just a block away. His jawline felt sick, puffy. The lymph nodes there were bumpy and tender. He made a spit bubble and yawned to make it pop.

That day at Food Kingdom, with a pocked face, Jeremy sacked groceries with a new kind of focus. He seemed to be more in touch with his hands, how they moved. There was that roundness to his peripheral vision, too, which made him slightly dizzy. His teeth felt funny and there was a stirring in his nether regions.

That night, Jeremy made sure the windows were closed to keep out whatever was biting him. The raised areas on his face made him feel ugly. It was bad enough being a 47-year-old sacker, and now this. He perused a beat-up copy of *Dolphins* by Jacques Yves Cousteau and fell asleep with the light on. He awoke at midnight and turned it off.

The next morning, Jeremy struggled out of bed. He felt stiff. His teeth—he could see his teeth protruding beneath his nose, which seemed to have flattened and hardened. He had to pee and waddled to the bathroom. In the mirror his face was covered with bites, on his cheeks, his forehead. He had trouble focusing, as if his eyes no longer communicated with one another. "Damn!" He had begun volunteering at the STD clinic and was in love with a nurse's aide there named Debbie Dee. She had said that she was on Mugbook, that they should be friends. It had taken Jeremy a few days to figure out what Mugbook was, that he would need a computer, and now this—"Dammit to hell!"

The bicycle locked to the fence outside his apartment looked foreign to Jeremy. It caused a vague sense of dread. The world had taken on a definite sphericity, and he wondered at his lack of hunger and thirst. He imagined that he was absorbing water from the atmosphere around him. He could "see" carbon dioxide in the air, especially the warm, moist CO_2-rich air of human exhalation.

Mr. Tippy, the manager of Food Kingdom, gave him a queer look as he struggled to tie his red full-length apron. He spoke to Jeremy, but Jeremy heard only dull whooshes interspersed with silence. He felt that his penis was hard and rod-like and that he needed to retract it.

Jeremy may have sacked groceries for a few minutes or maybe not. He wasn't sure. He tried to speak and tell Mr. Tippy that he needed to take the day off, to figure things out, to see what the hell was going on in his pants. He heard squeaks coming from his mouth, air being blown through a straw. The bites on his face and legs throbbed.

Jeremy found himself in his bed, on his back, staring at the textured ceiling. It looked like a disco ball and he darted his eyes to make the images tumble and realign. He turned his head and looked down at his body. He was turning a reddish, golden brown. His knees were stuck together, his elbows fixed to his ribs. Beneath the slope of his thorax, he could see his knife-like penis elongated and enfolded into his abdomen. It unfolded and extended. The tip was razor sharp and hollow.

He thought about Debbie Dee. If only he could see her! God, but what would she think? He struggled to remember. He had only this image of Debbie Dee, a frozen image, as if she were bending over him, her apple breasts surging outward, cold sores in the corners of her mouth. He slept.

In the morning, the room was terribly bright. He rotated his eyes, seeking a dark place. Hands now protruded from his chest, or rather stick-like remnants, jointed things with hairlike appendages. A set of the very same extended from his hips, and where his feet used to be, yet another. He tried to stand but could not and waved his "legs" in the air. The ceiling seemed a million miles away. He had to find Debbie Dee before it was too late. He rolled off the bed, landing on his "feet," which snagged in the carpet. Carefully he lifted each foot and made his way to the dim living room to wait for darkness.

~

On a can of hairspray in Debbie Dee's bathroom, detectives read this: Bedbugs reproduce through a process of traumatic insemination. The male pierces the female's abdomen with his penis (sword) and disperses sperm throughout the female's abdominal cavity.

Home Invasion!

Virgins before and after the break-in nine months earlier, sisters Aureola and Aurora gave birth to identical twins, a total of four boys, all in the spitting image of the sisters' father Duane, who had lost a testicle during the melee.

~

It was a bright night, the moon pressing down with a thousand faces upon Pianotown. Darkness curled beneath the eaves, behind brick walls, and at the bottoms of empty swimming pools, a soupçon of sweet hairspray in the chill air.

Inside the faux log cabin at 48 Wiffle Lane, a single light shone upstairs in the master bedroom. It was the mother, reading *Foxe's Book of Martyrs*. She was thin and wispy, but kept a tidy hearth and managed the house accounts with a flair for saving. Beside her slept the sisters' father, his arm curled over his face to block the light from the lamp. He suffered from psoriasis and a thick tongue, which protruded when he slept.

Fresh from the bus station, a man named HR with slick black hair, torn work pants, and wearing an old pair of combat boots, walked with purpose. He crossed in front of the yellow court house, which looked green in the moonlight, and passed the hairspray factory headed into the dark night, the heels of his shoes thudding. A dog barked from a backyard as he eased his way into the neighborhood. A curtain opened and closed. A porch light switched on.

Aureola and Aurora lay in their twin beds facing one another. The room was small. A very large wardrobe purchased from a flea market covered the near wall. Soft moonlight through an open window fingered the sheets. A bulky shadow of leaves leapt on the wall in silence. Both snored ever so lightly in thin yellow nightgowns. A cat lay curled behind Aureola's knees.

In the next bedroom, the mother listened to the rustle of the holly bush against the vinyl siding. There was a dog barking, perhaps two houses down. She read on, turning the page.

HR looked down as a motorist in a station

wagon passed. He needed a place to stay.
He needed money. He was hungry. A can of
hairspray caught his eye, leaning next to a
mailbox post. Printed on the plastic cap he
read this: Tonight you shall be responsible
for impregnating two sisters, but you will
not be the father. Be violent, take no pris-
oners, and make sure there's a bullet in the
chamber before you climb the ladder.

He scanned the house to his left, saw an
aluminum extension ladder on top of two
sawhorses, and broke open the barrel of his
.22 revolver. He nodded to himself and the
gun clicked shut. He mimicked the sound
with his tongue and stepped into the grass.

The mother put her book down, imagining
she heard the rattle of an extension ladder.
The dog was still barking. She sat in bed,
pondering what to do. Should she wake her
husband? There was a distinct bump against
the house. She touched Duane on the shoulder. "Hey," she whispered. "Hey!"

Duane's hand slid and he seemed to be
traveling from a far-away dream. He struggled to open his eyes and realized that
his wife was shaking him by the shoulder.
"What is it? Am I awake?" He turned to his
back.

"There's a noise in the yard. The Swanson's dog is barking, too. Could you check the girls' room, make sure they're okay?" *Foxe's Book of Martyrs* fell to the floor.

"Heard what?" He sat up rubbing his itchy elbows webbed with patchy red and inflamed skin. He focused and listened. A scratching sound, a kind of squeaking.

At the top of the ladder, HR peered into the bedroom. The window was open eight inches. The screen came out with ease and he let it drop to the grass below. He felt an excitement in his throat, in his testicles. He had never fathered a child. Perhaps that was what was missing in his life. He'd tried religion, most recently Catholicism, but had found it lukewarm. He reached in to raise the window higher.

Aureola and Aurora stirred in their sleep. The cat's head rose and pointed toward the window. The window was sliding up, the cool breeze becoming larger, fluttering the polka dot curtains.

HR pressed against the sill and propelled his body into the room. He tried to flip but landed sideways, hitting the corner of Aureola's bed. He reached for his pistol and stifled a sneeze.

The father Duane leapt from bed, looking from window to door. His heart beat wildly, thumping. It seemed to take up his whole chest. Aureola screamed. There was shouting. Duane grabbed the lamp and jerked it from the wall. He ran to the hall.

"Oh dear God," said his wife. She stood by the bed, gripping the dark red spread.

Aureola fled to the corner of her room. "Aurora!" she screamed. "Daddy!"

Into the room flew Duane. He flipped on the light and at the same time threw the lamp at the figure by the window, a man with slick black hair and a scowl. The lamp sailed over his shoulder and slammed the wall. The man looked violent, poised, and was holding a pistol.

Aurora stumbled from bed toward her sister. She grabbed her by the waist, pulling her, shielding her. Aureola was the youngest by three minutes.

"What the hell do you want!" said Duane. With the pistol trained on him, he walked in front of his daughters, arms spread as if he could catch bullets. He was in his underwear, which were inside out and dingy.

HR realized what he had to do and knelt on a small oval rug. With a steady hand, he aimed at Duane's scrotum, imagined the testicles hanging down. He felt a thrill and pulled the trigger, the bullet passing through HR and then Aureola and Aurora.

Dung Beetles Help the Elderly

from the *Pianotown Register*:
Dr. Truman Hallway Jr. knows constipation.
He oversees patients at the Pianotown nursing home and has over twenty years of experience "cleaning" his patients' "pipes."

We visited this week with Dr. Hallway
as he described his recent work using dung
beetles to relieve severe cases of locked bowels. He's a quiet man with dark hair streaked
with gray and wears a white lab coat with
his name stitched in red over a pocket full of
pens and a tiny flashlight.

The "facility," as he likes to call it, smells
of pine, but his own office smells of manila
folders and cold steel. On top of a bank
of green file drawers are three ten-gallon
aquariums. Inside are dozens of robust black
dung beetles, scurrying back and forth.

"I was camping down on Cumberland
Island one summer and saw some dung beetles on one of the trails. They were pushing
balls of horse s~~t to their burrows. At the
time I was constipated and put two and two
together."

In a bright room near the nursing station in the east wing, Dr. Hallway demonstrates his "feces breaking" zootechnology. Lying in bed is long-time resident Verlaine Spradley. She's about as wrinkled as they come but still retains the pleasant smile of yesterface. Dr. Hallway joked that "she could use a good ironing."

"Good morning, Verlaine," says Dr. Hallway. He takes her hand in his. "Is your tummy still hard?"

Verlaine looks from Dr. Hallway to the rectangle of window and sighs. "I'm froze up, doctor. I sure could use some help. Maybe some Epsom salts."

At this, Dr. Hallway brightens and pulls a Mason jar from his roomy lab coat pocket. "I've got the cure for what ails you right here, Verlaine."

"I sure appreciate it," says Verlaine squinting her cloudy eyes at the jar.

Nursing assistant Debbie Dee McClintock moves in to tie Verlaine's hands to the bed rails. "Open up wide, honey," she says to the frail but sturdy resident.

Into her mouth goes a rather large flexible tube the diameter of a quarter [see photo]. Verlaine gags and thrashes, but Debbie Dee is there to reassure her. "It's alright honeybear. Your sugar pie Debbie Dee is right here with you sweetie."

"Now for the magic," says Dr. Hallway. With forceps he withdraws a wriggling dung beetle and places it into the tube. The rotund bug slips down the tube, as if in a hurry. "The beetle can smell the clogged feces in her large intestine," he says. "It's just a matter of hours before the helpful insect reaches the impaction site and begins to burrow."

Verlaine's eyes are wide with excitement and she chokes, but the oxygen in her nose keeps her from turning blue.

We asked the doctor, "How long will it take for the patient here to experience relief?"

After inserting three dung beetles into the tube, he screws on the lid. "Oh, about twelve hours on average."

"Do the beetles survive the journey?"

"Oh, yes," says Dr. Hallway. "They come out a little soft from the digestive juices but fat and sassy nonetheless. I'd venture to say that they enjoy helping others."

He washes his hands, and Debbie Dee removes the tube from Verlaine's throat and unties her hands. Verlaine gags and coughs for a few minutes. "I'll kill you, you goddamn bastard!" she says.

The doctor and his assistant chuckle, knowing that constipation goes hand in hand with irritability.

Academic Team

Timothy held his buzzer like a packaged yellow sponge cake, thumb on the button. He wore tight corduroy pants, a white short-sleeve shirt, and glasses. He looked functional. He lived at Child Heaven, the orphanage north of Pianotown. His adopted parents did not necessarily like him but they encouraged his participation in the middle school's academic team, as long as creationism remained a central tenet of his belief system.

The moderator read the next question: "Be sure and duck under the ladder. In the previous sentence, which word is a homonym for a type of water bird?" She paused, pooching her lips, scanning the two tables of middle schoolers.

Timothy buzzed in. "There were two ducks on Noah's Ark."

"Incorrect. The answer is just 'duck.' Next question. And, Timothy, please wait to be identified before answering."

Concerned looks crossed adult faces in the quiet library. A chair scraped. The match was close, 12 to 11, in favor of the visitors from Pantsville Middle. Timothy scratched his head. His "dad" liked to put him in a headlock and make his head turn red.

"Hot as a two-dollar pistol is an example of an overused expression of speech. What word describes such expressions?" The moderator noticed a bit of dandruff on her glasses.

Timothy buzzed in.

"Timothy, Pianotown," said the moderator.

"There were no pistols in the Garden of Eden."

"Incorrect. The answer is cliché."

Timothy nodded, acknowledging his failure but remaining strong in his faith.

The moderator shifted her hips and turned the page. "This type of writing uses stanzas and rhymes. An example is 'The Raven' by Edgar Allen Poe."

Timothy blurted out the answer. "On Noah's Ark, the ravens were kept next to the doves."

"I'm sorry, you did not buzz in," said the moderator. *Buzz* went the buzzer. "Katrina, Pantsville."

"Poetry," said Katrina.

"Correct, Pantsville. Next question: How many species of animals did Noah take on the Ark?”

Buzz. “Timothy, Pianotown.”

“Twenty-three million, six hundred forty-three thousand, four hundred and nine.”

“That is correct.”

The timer indicated that the game was over. Ultimately, Timothy had lost the game for his team but did retain creationism as a central tenet of his belief system.

Birthday Cake

Birthday cake, birthday cake. Oh boy, birthday cake!

Weston sat in his highchair with his big bulbous head doddling. He was twice the size of an infant his age. Francine scratched her hindparts and poked a finger into the sugary icing, broke the crust, and made a hole.

A vague white light filled the small kitchen and made the brown floor look browner. There was a magnet on the refrigerator from Dollywood.

"Was that necessary?" said Weston. "You scratched your arse and then poked the cake." He was gravely articulate for his young age. He cooed like a pigeon.

Francine looked like a poorly drawn picture, her black hair jagged and sketchy. She let the dog Oodles lick her finger. In his excitement, Oodles dribbled pee on the floor.

"Oh, there goes Oodles," said Weston. "You're a bad boy!" He wagged his finger and sighed.

"Well, he's a good dog otherwise," said

Francine. "You want some more of this cake. It's real good."

"Well, it is a possibility," said Weston. "But it's your birthday. Your cake. I would hate for mummy to think me greedy."

"Oh hell, she's dead, boy."

"But, she's watching with God as He counts the sparrows…Mummy is gone. True." Weston reached and adjusted the latex of his diaper. "She had the most glorious milk. I can still taste it."

Francine grabbed a dirty sponge and wiped at a coffee ring on the laminate counter. She looked at the old Westinghouse clock on the wall. "Daddy will be home soon, and I can get the hell out of here. Have to fry damn porkchops and make beans for the old man."

"Oh, the unexamined life," said Weston. "Yours is one of quiet desperation." He yawned, making a snot bubble.

"Oh, shut your trap, big mouth. You say the most confounded things. I think you need to go outside and crawl with the dog. Come on, big boy." She loosened the tray on his highchair.

"Careful now with Weston," said Weston. He hugged her neck, smelling stale hair.

Francine hobbled to the back door with Weston on her hip. She looked like an S. She walked through the spidery laundry room to the outside door and pushed onto a ridiculously small deck. It was sprinkling, a pale yellow light as if the clouds held urine. "Gonna get you wet, boy."

"Really? Already I'm cold. Take me back inside." Weston pressed his head to her neck.

"Goddamn, you're heavy. You can crawl in the doghouse with Freckles." Freckles was all muscle, a chest like a freight train.

"I would give that a big no," said Weston.

"Shut up." She shifted her hip out even further, looking like a Z.

She walked into the patchy yard. In the far corner next to a pile of whitewall tires was Freckles' doghouse. Big piles of poop. There was a junk tree, a Chinese magnolia. Freckles strained at his chain, grinning like a monkey, whining, slobbering.

"I hate you," said Weston. He pinched Francine's flabby arm.

"Hey! You little dick." She pushed past Freckles and fairly dropped Weston onto the bare brown dirt. He clung to the bottoms of her red culottes, and she kicked him away. "Go on, get in there and get dry." She wiped rain from her face. She smelled diesel.

On hands and knees, Weston wept, his

wispy red hair blowing in the cool breeze. Francine kicked his bottom, sending his face into the dirt. There was newspaper caught in the chain-link fence.

"For God's sake, you bitch!" said Weston. He turned to his bottom, watching Francine walk away, his tears mingling with the rain that burned his eyes.

Freckles gave up straining against his chain and turned his attention to Weston, sniffing his face, licking his tears. Weston just let him, losing his balance and tipping over. He thought about the birthday cake, about his dead mother. His father would be home soon from the hairspray factory. Lying like a corpse, he noticed his foot planted in a pile of Freckle's poo. There were worms in the poo, wiggling white and tiny, hook-worms. A worm with Weston's name on it wangled between his toes and burrowed through the skin, making its way to a small vein. The rush of blood carried the worm to Weston's heart, pushing it into the small vessels of his lungs. Soon, Weston began to cough, and the worm crawled up the back of his throat. Weston swallowed and the worm made its way to his intestines where it latched on, sucked blood, and began to lay eggs.

At 5:10, Carl appeared in the street,

home from the factory. Rain peppered him, his hair a wet Q on his forehead. He was tall and cross-eyed, wearing his blue uniform with patches on the knees. Crossing the street, he kicked a can of hairspray and cursed. Out of habit, he picked up the can and read this: "Now, Freckles *and* Weston have worms. You're next. Oh, and Francine is 56, not 43." He threw the can into the storm drain and stepped onto the creaky porch. Dammit to hell if he was gonna get worms. Mommy had gotten worms. He thought about her milk and pushed through the dirty door into the tiny front room. He smelled old saltine crackers.

"Francine!" He stepped over a pile of cheap blankets. Worms lived in the stomach.

Francine was frying the damn porkchops. "Hey!"

Carl walked in. "Where's Weston, birthday girl?" He eyed her saggy butt.

"Oh, he's out back. He wanted to play in the rain with Freckles." Francine tapped her thigh with the greasy spatula.

"Worms live in the stomach," said Carl. He dipped his finger into the birthday cake, licked, and walked into the bedroom to get the .22.

Fat College Girls

Reynolds Macadoo had never had sex and decided that he would set about to correct that. He'd go to the Red Wagon and maybe get a fat girl drunk. He'd heard that the college girls put duct tape over their nipples in case their boobs fell out. He rubbed his hands together as if about to select a fine cheese. It had been another long day at the hairspray factory, plus he had spent that morning writing encouraging letters to missionaries.

Reynolds was tall and had a humped nose, from which he plucked tiny black hairs with tweezers that belonged to his grandmother. He stepped onto the crooked sidewalk and saw the phone dangling in the phone booth. He replaced it and read a new bit of graffiti: Rhino horn is for the birds. Three streets over he could see the giant cat that belonged to the pregnant woman who now lived in a giant coffee can. The giant litter box she'd lived in was up for rent.

He whistled as he walked, wearing his dark brown uniform. He passed the yellow court house on his way home, stopping to admire a nickel on the sidewalk, but it was heads down. He crossed the street, and in the road was a can of hairspray. He picked it up and read this: "When she tells you to get lost, she means in her pubic hair." He gave the can a couple of sprays and dropped it on the asphalt.

At his apartment he undid the wonky knob that held his door closed and let himself in. He stepped over the aquariums filled with hermit crabs and went to the kitchen for a cold glass of lemonade. He decided to rest his eyes, and soon fell asleep on the ragged brown couch, dreaming of pubic hair. When he awoke, it was half past seven, and he went to take a shower. He stepped in ever so slow, careful not to step on the hermit crabs.

It was only a five-minute walk to the Red Wagon. There was a red wagon outside the front door, which meant that they were open. He touched the hump on his nose and stepped inside, noting the smell of fried food and something like hibiscus. He looked around for fat college girls and only saw young men with scraggly beards and a few prim professors from the community college or maybe they were from the barber school.

The U-shaped bar was open on the left

side, and Reynolds took a barstool there. Right away, an older man pulled up beside him, reeking of industrial glue. It was Father McGlawn from the Unitarian "Church."

"Didn't expect to see you here," said Father McGlawn. He wore an old wool coat, buttoned up the front and had the face of a patient donkey.

"Well, jiminy crickets," said Reynolds. He'd felt a stiff hair on his nose and touched it. "I'm here to get laid. I've never had sex before."

"Well, that's what you've been telling everyone," said Father McGlawn. "It might be best to pretend otherwise, for maximum firepower, if you know what I mean." He ducked his head into his coat and took a big sniff.

The idea of firepower resonated with Reynolds. Often, when he masturbated, his bodily fluids would shoot onto his nipples.

"What can I get you?" said Alicia, the bartender. She touched her plastic hair with the deep part. She looked fresh from a Sears catalog.

"Oh, the usual," said Reynolds, trying to be original.

"I've never seen you before," said Alicia, "except walking in town."

Father McGlawn suggested he try a triple Jaeger bomb, and Reynolds nodded his approval.

"So, how was the service on Sunday?" said Reynolds. He saw a tiny flag on the wall near some bottles and saluted.

Father McGlawn yawned. "Oh, everyone was talking about the two hitchhikers duct-taped to mechanic's creepers in James's (Dr. Hartman's) basement. That eventually led us to the fall of the Roman Empire."

"Yeah, I read about them in the *Register,*" said Reynolds. "Not the Romans."

Alicia plunked down his triple Jaeger bomb mixed with ginger ale. "That'll be three camels and a duck."

Reynold's pulled out a five.

"I said, and a duck.'"

Reynold's pulled out a fifty.

"You need change?" said Alicia, or can I donate this to the nursing home?

Reynold's mother and father were in the nursing home. He put the change in his pocket and looked around at the men, no girls. "When do the fat college girls get here?"

Father McGlawn yawned. "They usually trot in half an hour before closing to mop up the extras."

"Jeez, that will be hours," said Reynolds. He downed half of his cluster bomb and belched. "Tastes like Listerine crossed with a Christmas tree." He touched the hump on his nose.

"That's a good one," said Father McGlawn. "A good arrangement of words."

For the next five hours, pretty college girls came and went, swizzling their Long Island Tea and Sex on the Beach. Father McGlawn nursed a robust ale, watching Reynolds swimming toward an alcohol oblivion. He raised his eyebrows when an attractive young blonde put her hand on Reynolds shoulder and called him by name.

Thoroughly clocked, Reynolds turned his head and could only focus on the wall beyond where hung patches and pennants. She wore a tube top with MOTOR BOAT ACADEMY emblazoned across her chesty chest. Her name was Debora, her nickname Deboralicious, and she was a cosmetics counter major at the community college.

"Well, hey," said Reynolds. His eyes crossed, and a loud one crept from his behind. Father McGlawn coughed and held his beer to his breast.

"You're Reynolds Macadamia Nut," said Debora. I saw you in *Hermit Crab Magazine*. They're free at the hardware store." She touched her pointy nipples to his back. "I have eleventeen hermit crabs in my dorm

room. I was impressed with how you rotate
your crabs from the tub, to cardboard boxes,
and then back again. It's quite the diversity
of application." She spit just a little when
she talked, her long blonde hair shimmery
bouncy wow.

Reynolds telescoped his eyes in and out,
seemingly on stalks. Someone or something
was pushing ripe strawberries into his back.
He checked his watch, an hour to go till
closing. "I'm just waiting on the fat girls to
get here." He motioned to Alicia for another
drink.

"Oh, yucky yuck," said Deboralicious.
She gave Father McGlawn a dollar and
moved on to a passel of young men waiting
to pee.

Mission Work

Jamie banged on the warped door. The painted doorknob felt like rubber. The battleship-gray porch sagged in the middle. He was tired of pretending to drive junk cars. He wanted a Hostess Ho Ho, the ones in the shiny, paper-thin foil. His mama was taking a bath and wouldn't let him in.

Jamie smoked brown Winchesters. He walked in the side door of Hazelnut's, picked up a six-pack of empty Orange Crush bottles, and walked around to the register. Mr. Hazelnut with his little gray mustache gave him thirty cents. Jamie pointed at the Winchesters and kept the nickel. On the way out, he stole a Chic-o-Stick.

"There's a gang gathered up to kill our cuss-ed selves," said Robert. The brown fuzz on his upper lip made it all seem real to Jamie. Robert's mama dated. His uncle drank cooking sherry, whatever that was. There was a cockroach frozen into the icy lip of the refrigerator freezer. One of the best days was when Robert's grandpa fell through the rotten floor and broke his foot.

Robert and Jamie gathered rocks into
piles. There would be nunchucks, bazookas,
and eighty-pound radios. Red Man dripped
down Robert's chin. Jamie climbed a tree,
smoked three Winchester's, and spotted the
enemy descending upon them in chariots
of vinegar-blue commanded by naked boys
with sharp throats and kicked eyes. A cricket
hidden in the morning glory sang out.

Between Robert's house and Jamie's sat
a sad little crackerbox house with a Rambler
squatting in the red dirt around back. Jamie
smashed the little windows with a steel milk
crate. The Rambler repelled rock after rock
with crisp cracks and hollow bonks. They
didn't have a gun so they couldn't shoot the
old couple who lived inside eating cold Pop-
Tarts and runny eggs.

Jamie shot up the power meter with his
BB gun. Every night, he dreamed about a
man with cartoon teeth hiding in the house.
After his bath, Jamie always sat in front of
the electric heater until the towel smoked.
The TV roared like sand, but he turned it on
anyway. He had a baseball glove but what
the hell could he do with it? He wanted to
break his arm so bad he could taste it.

Dusty Turnipseed from the orphanage
stole Jamie's glasses. Jamie told the teach-
er and felt bad when Dusty handed them

over. More than once Dusty came to school with bloody socks, his backside a mess. He smelled like piss. He needed somebody to kill him and make him easy. Jamie smashed the glasses with a two-by-four and threw them in the woods.

Jamie grew up and took an airplane to Africa. Everybody in Pianotown took a deep breath and said that despite our constant lack of faith, God always looks after his own.

22

Pianotown is nowhere. An old Pepsi billboard leans toward traffic along the state
highway running through it. Decorum
Feather, a nice young lady with hay fever
and full lips, lives there, coughs, is nauseous
at times, is sensitive to the weather, especially rain, rainbows, rainbows in the sky,
gasoline rainbows. She wears soft blue jeans
during the week with print shirts, plaids,
paisley, pumpkins on Halloween. The jeans
are folded at night and laid on a maroon
velvet-seated chair, belt in the loops, worn
for the week's entirety barring some potting
soil incident; and a dress on Sunday, print
dresses with sashes. She would like to have
someone tie the sash from behind. Saturdays
depend, could be a tube top. Feather is bi-
lingual, able to chat with the migrant work-
ers from El Salvador who pick red tomatoes
from green vines.

Cars are bought and sold in Pianotown.
There are churches and groceries. It's not
a bad place to live nor a bad place to visit.
Clouds frequent the sky. The ground re-

ceives rain, parsing the overflow into rivu-
lets, streamlets, brooks, creeks, and a small
river. Water from the tap is memorable,
sweet. The county is dry, but cooking sherry
is available at Food Kingdom. That could be
changing soon.

Decorum Feather works in a flower shop.
She snips roses and floats them in bowls.
Above the flower shop is an apartment
where lives Peter Hudgins. He's harmless,
not unattractive, but suffers from anxiety
and depression. Decorum would like for
Peter to look her way, feeling in her bones,
especially her legs, the long leg bones, an
ache there, that she could be of use to Peter.

Walking in a light rain, her clogs plash-
ing, Decorum sees a can of hairspray and
bends down. The can is covered with rain.
In a small font beneath a barcode, she reads
this: "No more pumpkins for you, sister.
Peter is into stock car racing. Approach him
wearing a bright red shirt with the number
five or forty-three on it. Make your voice
growl like an engine."

That's it. She has a plan and veers left
to the thrift store. The thrift store is bright,
has no dressing room, and smells like stale
cloth. Inside she finds a jersey with the
number 22 on it. It's black and red and costs
two dollars. Hopeful, she returns home and

tries it on, sneezing.

The next day, Arbor Day, a tornado rips through Pianotown, taking out the old folks home. Numerous dung beetles have escaped. Old people have died, sucked into nearby pastures, sprawled in the median of the highway missing their teeth, some still with houseshoes. During the tornado, Peter Hudgins has hurried down to the flower shop, seeking refuge.

Beneath a table covered with glass vases and spools of ribbon, Decorum finds herself thigh to thigh with Peter along with an old man with a long nose.

"Say, the number 22," says the old man. "What is that, hockey?"

"Sure as hell ain't NASCAR," says Peter. "Won't catch me supporting Team Penske."

"Oh," says Decorum. "I meant to buy number five or forty-three. I'm sorry. The hairspray, you know."

Peter laughs. "Now you're talking my language. Say, you work here don't you?"

The old man says, "No, I do not."

"Not you, the missus," says Peter.

"Yes, I've always worked here," says Decorum in a growly voice.

The tornado passes overhead, removing the roof. A downspout cartwheels through the street with an old tire, then several cans of hairspray. Pushing along with a wave of water is a hitchhiker duct-taped to a car creeper.

"My, you tickle my fancy," says Peter. "I've never noticed you before. So you like the races?"

"What races?" says the old man. His long nose drips clear fluid.

"Oh, I think he means me," says Decorum and then she says, "Grrr."

"Well hotdog!" says Peter. "I think this tornado business is about over. I hope my posters didn't get wet."

The howling has abated, a vacuum. The three crawl out on their hands and knees, standing.

"Well, listen baby cheeks, I'd love to take you to the corner store and buy you some barbecued butt. What you think?"

"I'm a vegetarian," says Decorum. She brushes her sleeves.

"Hell," says Peter. "The hairspray told me to run from the vegetable lady, that she was just intent on playing my harp strings willy nilly."

"Oh," says Decorum. "Can I help you gentlemen with any flowers?"

The old man nods. "Yes, daises, yellow ones for my dumpling. We met fifty years ago over a can of hairspray. But things have changed. Just the other day, a can told me to put razor blades in my shoes. What the hey? So, it's sad, but the cans just don't have the same pull as they used to."

Decorum lets a single tear escape her left eye, watching as the giant cat walks through the rubble outside.

Spoke To

Ermaletta was a nurse, an LPN, and she liked to kill her patients for no good reason. Sometimes it was the way they coughed or combed their hair.

Inside the nursing home, Ermaletta drug slow down the hallway, patting poor old Mrs. Betsy on her white head. "Good old Betsy," said Ermaletta. She would never kill her. She wasn't in her right mind, and it didn't seem fair.

Bored to tears, she saw the light blinking for number 47, Mr. Claude Stumps. He was next on the list, and she sashayed that way, her rumpus heaving up and down. She walked in and Claude was sitting on a bedside commode, his head in his hands as if in deep prayer. He was frail but still had thick hair.

"You done hocked a big one," said Ermaletta. She patted her double belly, little ringlets of red hair beside her small ears.

Claude spread into a toothless grin, ashamed. "Help me out, sister. Get me back to bed."

"Do you need wiping?" Ermaletta posed with hands on hips, her little Timex tick, tick, ticking.

"Do I have to beg?" said Claude.

"I'd like to see you beg," she said in a whisper, looking over her shoulder. She popped on a glove and wound toilet paper around her right hand, her wiping hand. "Raise up, old timer."

Claude grimaced and leaned forward.

"I said raise up. You deaf?" She said deef.

"Oh, to hell with you. I'll just sit here and rot."

Ermaletta noticed a can of hairspray on the floor. She picked it up and read the tiny letters. "Reach beyond the moment. Is it really worth your time killing these old codgers? Man up and put some lead between your eyes." Ermaletta dropped the can, deep dark thoughts running through her tiny head.

"Uh, yes sir," said Ermaletta. She plunged her hand down his backside and wiped him three times, smearing shit on the toilet seat. "I gotta go and sit down. I done been spoke to." She pulled the glove over the soiled paper and let it drop in the waste bin. "You have been marked by angels."

"Well, ain't no angel I've seen. Get me back in bed. I'm awful tired of sitting here."

Claude was kind of purple, his lips blue. He breathed through his mouth. He'd smoked for sixty years, but that was done.

"Yes, sir," said Ermaletta and she half hauled him onto the bed and threw a sheet over him. "Now get some shut eye and don't be pressing that button. You hear me?"

"I'll press it if I damn well want to," said Claude. The sheet was up to his chin. "I'm cold, Ermaletta. Cover me up, Ermaletta."

But Ermaletta was out the door into the pale green hall. She could hear Mr. Pansy shouting from his room about World War Two. Another LPN, Charlotte, was walking her way.

"You look like you done been swallowed," said Charlotte. She chewed gum, which was against the rules.

"I've been spoke to," said Ermaletta.

"You mean them damn hairspray cans? Found one in my yard yesterday. Told me not to let little Jimmy play with firecrackers. He was sure tore up when I took away his bottle rockets."

"You did the right thing, sweetie," said Ermaletta.

"Said something else too. Didn't want to mention it to you."

Ermaletta paled, paler than pale, the corpuscles in her face shrinking. "What, dear, what? Tell me, sweetie."

"Said to buy a new dress for the funeral."
She ran her finger across her throat.

Ermaletta shuddered. They'd just hire
another LPN and nobody would miss poor
old Ermaletta.

"Well, that's that," said Charlotte. "Gotta
give a bath to Mr. Hoskins. You okay?"

"You sure it said Ermaletta on the can?"

Charlotte nodded, lying through her
teeth.

Ermaletta knew what she had to do.

The Door

Jean and Truman decided to visit Pianotown, after hearing of a young hirsute who choked on her own hairball. They were especially touched by news that donations in her memory would benefit the wild horses of Kansas. In preparation, they hired an elderly neighbor to watch their cat and pigeon, returned overdue library books, and emptied the dishwasher. The drive from Langley Air Force Base took eight hours and fourteen minutes in their maroon minivan.

Jean was obtuse with a sharp nose. She favored a pair of worn jeans, usually paired with an old flannel shirt from a previous marriage. Her husband Truman was tall and gangly, wore black-frame glasses, and sported a track suit around the house. It had been ages since their last vacation to Blowing Rock (Rick), North Carolina, and this trip had them on edge with anticipation.

Turning from the interstate, the first thing they noticed was the giant cat, nearly twenty feet tall, stepping gingerly among the houses as if in a litterbox.

"Look, Truman, the giant cat," said Jean.

"Well, what the pumpkin guts?" said Truman.

They drove into town, passed the yellow court house, and within five blocks found the Pianotown Motor Lodge, which was next to the nursing home. A fine mist of hairspray drifted in the cool breeze.

The motor lodge was perfectly normal, an L of fourteen rooms, the outside painted white. Inside the office was an Indian man with bucked teeth. He was on chemotherapy for kidney cancer and looked sour. "Jī āiā nū," he said in Punjabi, followed by, "Do you have a reservation?"

"Oh, yes," said Jean. "The Barnswallows, Jean and Truman."

The Indian man flipped through a ledger and scribbled. He handed them a key attached to a red balloon. "The breakfast buffet is nice. Will you join us?"

"No," said Jean. "We brought our own food."

"And water," said Truman. He was getting an erection and didn't know why, although bucked teeth held a certain place in his heart.

They carted their luggage, tote bags, and cooler into number 12. The room was small, paneled in warm honeyed wood, and smelled of camphor. They settled in, sitting on the bed, wondering what to do next.

"There's that bar," said Jean.

"The Red Wagon," said Truman.

Within half an hour, after making love on the floor, they walked down Main Street past the hairspray factory. There was a man talking on a payphone who looked miserable. He had cold sores. They waited, and he stepped away from the phone leaving it dangling by the cord.

"Pardon us," said Truman. "We need directions to the Red Wagon."

"Oh," said the man. "Down one block and then take a left." He dabbed at the corner of his mouth with a tissue.

"Thank you," said Jean, knowing that the herpes virus caused depression.

Hand in hand they walked and soon came to the bright green door of the Red Wagon.

Truman paused and touched the door. "I've dreamed of this door." He handled the knob, feeling the slickness of a thousand hands before him. "Just look at the handiwork."

"Yeah, yeah," said Jean. "Just go in. None of this door foolishness."

Truman stared at the door, heavy and wooden with plate glass. A sign that said "Open." "This handiwork..." He touched the glass and then the knob again. "The trim. The paint. Wow."

Disgusted, Jean opened the door and disappeared inside.

Truman dug in his back pocket and retrieved his cell phone. He stood back and took a picture then posted it to Mugbook. He walked across the street and kicked a can of hairspray. He retrieved it from the gutter and read this: "That door needs your love."

Truman understood. He gazed at the door from his distance and walked toward it with a hitch in his gait, his hand in his pants. By the time he was able to touch it again, the sticky mess was in his underwear.

"Hail Mary," said Truman, and he pushed inside to join his wife for a drink.

One Thing and then Another

James (Dr. Hartman) knew that Adeline was alive but he declared her dead anyway. Maybe she would "sit up" at the funeral. He would go to see (just in case). Too bad about her unborn baby, though.

~

The first time James (Dr. Hartman) invited Adeline to his house, he did not introduce her to the two hitchhikers duct-taped to mechanic's creepers in his basement. He wanted to warm her up first, invite her to the Unitarian "Church," and maybe go out for a spaghetti dinner with all the fixings.

Adeline was one of those adequate types. She was neither attractive nor ugly. James (Dr. Hartman) thought of her as "serviceable" and "kind of cute," even with her wiry mop of brown hair. She'd been dating Henry at the hairspray factory, but that had cooled after Henry was struck by a meteorite. That and his constant cold sores. So, when James (Dr. Hartman) began chatting her up at the

Red Wagon, she was "ripe for the picking" as his father, long dead, would have said. Besides, even though James (Dr. Hartman) limped, he had a handsome chin and a lithe torso.

They began making love after watching old movies on the VCR player, but always used condoms. Adeline was prone to catalepsy and would often enter a catatonic state, which titillated James (Dr. Hartman). He enjoyed having his way with her while she slept the sleep of the damned. One night, however, after an intriguing episode of *Brother Cadfael,* they had passionate sex, initially with a condom, but as the night wore on, James (Dr. Hartman) felt that it would be safe to go natural. Little did he realize the potency and vigor of his own sperm.

Eight months into the pregnancy and facing "reality," James (Dr. Hartman) decided to do away with both Adeline and the baby. She did not approve of his gut racing hitchhikers in the basement, and she wanted to teach the infant baby sign language, which James (Dr. Hartman) thought ridiculous.

It was during *Jaws,* just as Adeline was beginning to come, that she blazed into one of her catatonic fits. She was stiff at first and mumbled with her eyes rolled back in her

head, but gradually relaxed and took on the
countenance of the deceased.

Putting Plan A into action, James (Dr.
Hartman) injected Adeline with a long-act-
ing barbiturate (phenobarbital), put blue
blush around her eyes, and dialed 911.
When the paramedics arrived, they took his
word (a doctor's word after all) that she was
dead and transported her the three blocks to
the Pianotown funeral parlor owned by his
brother Larry. Cooks covered their mistakes
with gravy and James (Dr. Hartman) covered
his with six feet of dirt. Her next of kin, all
in prison, were notified but were unable to
attend the service and burial, which James
(Dr. Hartman) arranged, Father McGlawn
attending.

Just before Father McGlawn closed the
thin wooden casket, Adeline gave birth, the
infant slipping between her thighs unseen.
Fortunately for James (Dr. Hartman), Doreen, who lived in a giant coffee can and who
was herself pregnant, was singing "Amazing
Grace" and no one heard the muffled cries.

~

In her grave, Adeline could hear the earth
thumping down on her coffin, but still remained locked in the latter stages of her
drugged and catatonic state (thanks to

James, *aka* Dr. Hartman). There was wetness and movement between her legs. She opened her eyes to darkness and the hardness of the wooden lid. A small pillow lay beneath her head and something soft beneath her body like a comforter.

Up top, the gravedigger sat in a small front-end loader with a bucket. He pushed the dirt sideways into the hole as a steady sprinkle of rain hardened into a regular spring shower. Not quite finished, he turned the loader back toward the shed, afraid of being struck by lightning.

Adeline felt the coffin around her. She tried to sit up and bumped her head. She tried again. She heard a mewling, a snuffling. She felt her abdomen and realized she'd given birth. Without light to guide her, she remained frozen, thoughts racing. She had been watching *Jaws* with James (Dr. Hartman) before everything went blank. She screamed. She recalled the hitchhikers in his basement and realized that he was capable of most anything. She had been blind, drawn in by his homemade wine, and won over by his friends at the Unitarian "Church."

A deep welling of motherly tenderness wrenched her from nightmarish musings. She moved her legs, tried again to sit up and cursed. She had a limited amount of air, *right?* and began to panic. How could she save herself?

The only way to bring the infant closer was to grab it by the hair and pull. It struggled and cried in heaving sobs. She felt between its legs and it was a boy. "John," she said. "My little John." The air in the coffin was hot, stifling. John nuzzled to her breast as she ripped open her plain white shirt with red buttons. She could feel his tears, his warm skin, his strong suck as he drew his first nourishment outside the womb. She thrust her elbows down and pushed her palms against the wood. She could feel the top move ever so slightly. John sucked madly, coming on and off her nipple. She drew up her knees. She pushed again. It was getting hard to breathe. She just wanted to hold John, to comfort him, but it looked as if they both would die. She screamed and beat the sides with her hands. Then she listened, but could only hear the slurping cries of John and his breathing, which seemed labored. She kicked and screamed for God to help her. Then she recognized the smell of earth and could feel the weight of dirt above her. If only she could break the cover and dig her way out. She needed a tool, something hard.

How many Philistines had Samson killed with the jawbone of an ass?

Adeline beat the coffin with her hands. She struggled to breathe. Little newborn John, screamed, racing chills down Adeline's sweat-soaked spine. It seemed they would perish, suffocate together, baby to mother's breast. The face of James (Dr. Hartman) swept across the blackness in red blurs. She cursed the day she had met him. She cursed the woman who had given birth to James (Dr. Hartman) and finally she cursed God. There was no time to lose.

While she strangled tiny John, she imagined looking in a mirror, fussing with her wiry brown hair. She looked like an uncombed monkey in the morning! Her mother had made her cry as a young girl, combing through the tangles.

There was silence. A warm thing slid from her chest to the side of the coffin, John. The sturdiest bones would be those of the legs.

With sticky hands, she gouged at the pine board, gouged, hammered, and pounded. There was a crack in the wood. She could feel it. She pressed up with her knees, gasping for breath. The lid split and down came earth as the boards separated and pressed against her. She turned to her side, keeping the remains of John within reach. Dirt filled her mouth, but there was a freshness of air, air trapped in the loose clods of dry earth. She had to let one half of the coffin top slip below her and then push up and out, but there was so much dirt. She dug and clawed at the soil until her fingers felt as if they were broken. There was a space for her head. She closed her eyes and took slow deep breaths through her nose. Dear God, she would need a tool to dig with, something bowl shaped—and she did what she had to do.

She whispered his name, "John, John, John." She swallowed dirt. She urinated. She coughed. She fashioned the skull and began to dig, her arms pushing up through the dirt.

Gravedigger Rusty Russell watched the robins listening and pecking at the remaining mound of dirt. He loved the way they cocked their heads, hearing the worms wiggle, rustling within the soil. He hadn't finished filling in the grave, the rain having stopped him with the threat of lightning, which he feared "more than hepatitis C."

Rusty had fair skin, blue veins along his jaw, and stood an even six feet, the same depth as the graves he dug. He sat atop the front-end loader, thinking about how he'd

run out of cream for his coffee that morning.
He'd tried some milk powder, but it wasn't
the same. The sky was moist and blue, a ten
o'clock sun climbing toward noon. Cicadas
cried like spoiled babies. There was another
hole to dig, this one in a potter's field for
a hitchhiker named Eddie Cavanaugh. He
had been sawed in half from his anus to his
mouth, but only halfway through the body.
The spectacle had everybody guessing.

Like a movie, he saw it. A finger, then
two fingers breaking through the crust of
red dirt. It looked kind of funny weird. The
dirt trembled around the fingers, a caving in,
a digging, and something white and bowl-
shaped appeared, stained by the red dirt.
He cut the engine and hopped down to the
green grass. He looked east toward a field
knee-high with soybeans. He could hear big
rigs in the distance heading down the highway. He was thinking about getting a smart
phone, one that would give him driving
directions.

Rusty took a shovel and began to push
the dirt away from the wiggling hands.
There were no rings that he could see. The
fingers were purple and bloody. He reached
down and squeezed one. With precision he
dug a shaft parallel to the arms, resisting the
urge to whistle.

Now standing upright surrounded by
earth, Adeline pushed up with her feet and
extended her arm. She felt a warmth, perhaps the sun. Just then her uterus cramped
and had she been able, she would have dou-
bled over. The placenta had yet to be born.
Was something touching her hand? She
heard a whoosh, a sliding sound, metal into
dirt. She was fully extended, standing on
top of the coffin, packed into the dirt, hands
reaching toward heaven.

Rusty said, "Zowie," and wiped sweat
from his eyebrows. He'd forgotten his straw
hat. He had little patches on his scalp,
"pre-cancers" that itched and flaked. The
top of a head had appeared and he used his
hands to scoop away the soil. This was going
to make a great story.

Before her face was fully exposed, Adeline began to weep with joy. She cried out,
"Eli, Eli! Lama sabachthani!" which confused Rusty. Was he not rescuing her?

With dirt-encrusted eyes, Adeline lifted
her face to the warm sun. Her eyes were
filled with dirt but she could see the light.
For the first time, she saw the digging tool
in her hand, and she resumed weeping,
this time with deep sorrow at what she had
done.

Rusty dug down to her shoulders, but

Adeline could not hoist herself from the shaft of earth that pressed her body. He could see the tops of her smeared breasts and felt a stiffening in his pants. "Up from the grave He arose," said Rusty.

"With a mighty triumph o'er his foes," said Adeline.

"He arose the victor from the dark domain."

"And lives forever with His saints to reign."

Rusty dug behind Adeline, careful not to scrape her back. It seemed that it was her hips keeping her in the hole. She clawed at the dirt around her chest. Now she was more or less topless and Rusty licked his lips.

With the help of a rope beneath her stubbly armpits, Adeline clawed her way from the hole that gripped her like a fist. She fell to her knees, exhausted, and at that moment birthed the overdue placenta. Rusty, the gravedigger, marveled at the glistening, maroon pancake of flesh flopped there in the green grass moist from the rain. The placenta was attached by the umbilical cord to what only could be called a bloody mess.

Up walked Boistrous Rainey from the Unitarian "Church," come for her daily walk among the tombstones. The site of Adeline,

living, breathing, and clutching at the gravedigger shocked her. Was Adeline not dead?
What was the gory mess in the grass? She
stepped closer for a look.

"Where is the head?" she asked. "It ap-
pears that the legs have been removed."

Still gripping the skull, Adeline held it
forth as explanation. She was covered in dirt
and mud, her face pale, her eyes vacant.

"Oh my. You were buried alive, gave birth
in the coffin, and then used the infant's
bones to dig your way out?"

Adeline nodded her head yes. She was
terribly thirsty. Her breasts hung full and
limp.

"Dear God, won't James (Dr. Hartman)
be surprised? Did you swallow dirt? Dirt has
nutrients." She helped Adeline button her
soiled blouse.

Rusty stood, dumbfounded, speechless.
He had another grave to dig. Should he
finish filling in the grave of Adeline? But
she was alive. He would need to speak with
Father McGlawn and quickly before the day
got away. "Let's get her into a chair or something," he said.

Together, he and Boistrous walked Adeline to the small chapel and sat her there
on a pew. She leaned forward to the pew in
front and began to heave with tears. Rusty

ran to his stone cottage and dialed the chief of police. He then took a few minutes and made tuna salad sandwiches cut diagonally and poured a glass of water. He stumbled outside and picked up a can of hairspray. On it he read this: "Adeline likes tuna salad but she does not like the crusts. Make sure you cut them off first." He went back inside, removed the crusts, and then returned to the chapel.

"See if she'll eat," he said.

"He sacrificed his life so that I could live," said Adeline.

"Just like Jesus," said Boistrous, although it was only a story to her. She sat beside Adeline and held out a sandwich.

"Do you have any carrot sticks?" said Adeline. She looked deep into the eyes of Boistrous.

"What you really mean is that you would like to eat the placenta and eat what's left of the child as well? To bring a symbolic end to its birth and death? I could see that it was a little boy. What was his name?"

"John," said Adeline. "Just John."

Rusty went to the shed to fetch the grill.

www.ingramcontent.com/pod-product-compliance
Lightning Source LLC
Chambersburg PA
CBHW032030180726
48284CB00008B/2540